I0525685

THE HONEYSUCKLE ANTHOLOGY

C. JAI FERRY

Copyright © 2014 C. Jai Ferry

All rights reserved.

This book or any portion thereof may not be reproduced or used in any manner whatsoever without the express written permission of the publisher, except for the use of brief quotations in a book review.

ISBN: 0615992455
ISBN-13: 978-0615992457

Inkwell International
87779 571 Avenue
Laurel, NE 68745

www.inkwellinternational.com

CONTENTS

PART I:

HONEYSUCKLE ROAD

PHILADELPHIA, 1964

We sit in the Special Room, crispy clean and only for pretty guests. Nana's in her overstuffed purple chair Granddaddy gave her before he died, and I'm on the wooden floor smelling the fresh polish and sucking on hard candy Nana's brought from work.

"Tell me about the bad baby boy," I say around a mouthful of cherry sugar. "Please." I know I got to speak real good with Nana.

"Oh, Donetta," Nana laughs, but it isn't an angry laugh. "I believe I told you that story just last night." I shrug and wait. She'll tell me again. "Should we find Teane and Wayne?"

I shake my head. I don't want my cousins to share none of my time with Nana. They interrupt Nana and try to change the telling so the bad people win. They think they too grown up for stories, anyways. "The bad baby boy." I suck on the candy until it becomes a piece of my tongue and I got to scrape it with my top teeth.

"All right then," Nana says and moves into her storytelling position. I copy her example. We sit with shoulders pulled up toward the ceiling, hands crossed in our laps. I move my skirt trying to hide my ugly legs, but my knees knot into the fabric.

"Once upon a time, there was a beautiful young woman who wanted very badly to have a child. But she hadn't been blessed with one and she thought something was wrong with her."

Nana looks out the large picture window. I know the beautiful woman would've looked just like Nana, but not with her tired eyes.

"So she went to the elder women and asked them why she couldn't have a baby. The women looked at her arms and legs, her head and her body. They couldn't find any problems so they told her to go to the village healer."

Nana waits for me. It's the same every night. I push the candy around in my mouth so I can talk like a lady, using my grown up voice. "What did the healer say?"

"Well, he could help her, but she might not get exactly what she wanted."

"But she really wanted a baby, right?" I smile showing my teeth and Nana laughs. Her laughter's a little bell, tickling behind my ears. She tells me I'm the prettiest child when I smile with teeth. I show her my teeth as much as possible.

"Yes, she was determined to have a baby. So the healer put his hand on her stomach and spoke in a very strange language. And do you know what happened?"

I start rolling my eyes, but Nana calls it an unladylike habit. "She got her baby."

"Yes, but not right away. She had to wait until it was time to harvest the crop. And when all the other women were in the fields, this woman had a little baby boy."

"And he cute, ain't he?" I lean forward with my elbows on my knees, my chin in my hands.

"Was cute, wasn't he," Nana says, looking down her nose at me.

"He was cute, wasn't he?" My stupid tongue gets me in a lot of trouble with Nana, but I been practicing. I just forget sometimes.

"He was the cutest baby ever born in the village. But when the women came back from the fields, they were afraid of the baby." Nana moves forward just the tiniest bit and I know she's going to share a secret. "They said he was evil."

"How'd they know?" I always ask the question, but I never get a real good answer. Evil babies must have purple eyes or square birthmarks, and I need to know what it is so I can check out Teane. Teane stays with me when Nana's cleaning the rich people's houses, but I think Teane is evil. She never tells me stories or sits with me on the porch. She's too busy standing by the street and flirting with boys, even the ugly ones.

"Women know about babies." It's how Nana always answers. "Well, this evil baby grew into a little boy and still the women were afraid of him. He never took baths. He spit in people's food. And when he was just about your age, he started to understand that the women didn't like him, and he laughed at them."

"They should've called his Nana. She would've taught him to be good." I swallow the last of the candy and feel the sugar sickness start in my stomach. "He must've been real lonely. I'd have played with him and showed him how to be good."

"The little boy went to a powerful healer and said he wanted to be stronger than the village women."

"Didn't the healer know he was evil?"

Nana slaps her hands on her knees and I put on my apology face just in case, but then she laughs. "Remember, Donetta, men aren't as smart as women in these matters. The healer was weak and he believed the little boy was being treated unfairly. So he gave the little boy a powerful amulet."

"The amulet, that's a black rock."

"Yes." Nana gives me the right-answer nod. "And what did he do with the amulet?"

"He put it around his neck."

"Very good."

Nana's head keeps bobbing and I sit up taller and taller until I am too tall and my shoulders fall back and my stomach punches forward. I fix myself before Nana sees.

"And he went back to the village and he did an awful thing." Nana's face is serious, and I push the corners of my mouth down to my chin, trying to copy her. "He destroyed all the women."

"Not all of them!" I don't like Nana's serious face. I want her to smile and tell me I'm right some more.

"No, not all of them," she says. "There was one old woman who lived outside the village and she had her own yellow amulet. And she came into the village to fight the little boy. And they fought and fought, but they were both very strong with their amulets."

"So who won?"

"Why don't you tell me?"

I got to finish the story the right way, the way she does, not like Wayne and Teane do. "God looked down from heaven and he saw what was going on and he wasn't happy. So he came down and he took both the little boy and the old woman back to heaven with him."

Nana nods. "And what about the amulets?" she says.

"They stayed in the village because God didn't want no fighting in heaven."

"Right, and now the yellow amulet controls daytime and the black amulet controls nighttime" Nana tilts her head.

"Which is why we got day and night." Nana claps her hands, and I stand up to make a curtsy, deep and low, eyes closed, like she taught me. She reaches into her skirt pocket and pulls out a candy, another cherry one, my reward for helping tell the story. I pop it in my mouth as she stands up, then take her hand and we walk out of the Special Room and back down the hallway into the boring rooms.

"You go play while I get dinner ready." Nana pulls my arm back and makes me look her in the eye. "But remember, no going off the porch."

"Yes, Nana." Nana doesn't like it when I pout, so I try not to show it, but if she'd let me go play with the neighborhood kids, then I wouldn't have no reason to pout. Nana says I'm too little and have to be careful. Wayne whispers to me that it's because my head's too big and my baby legs can't carry it correctly, and Nana's afraid I'll trip and fall and bust my head all over the sidewalk and she'll have to get down and clean it up. I don't want Nana cleaning up after me. She's already got knotty knees from waxing other people's floors.

Nana pushes me toward the door, but I have to ask. "Does anyone know where the village with the two amulets is?"

Nana looks at me like she looks at Wayne when he's trying to talk his way out of trouble. Maybe I shouldn't have asked.

"No, child," she says. "God doesn't want anyone to mess with day and night."

God doesn't want to have no more trouble like the bad baby boy. He's already got enough to do listening to everyone's prayers every night and before dinner. I walk out the door thinking about the healer living in the village with the amulets. Maybe he's got an amulet for my big head. Then Nana'll let me play anywhere on the block.

Nana's porch wraps around the front of the house and takes me nine giant steps to cross. But I like using sixty-eight baby steps instead. I watch kids play tag and chalk up the sidewalks. I can hear them playing, running, laughing, screaming in the rows of houses, but I don't see nobody. They never come play with me on my porch. There ain't enough room to laugh here. Three steps lead down to the front yard and I plop on the bottom step and stretch my feet as far out into the freedom of the grass as they go, which isn't very far.

I hear Wayne whistling that stupid song he always whistles. I think he does it just because he knows I hate it. He whistles the same song over and over, but he won't teach me to whistle, says I'm too little to whistle, not smart enough. Nana says ladies don't whistle. She doesn't say they don't know how to do it, they just don't do it, so I think it's okay for Wayne to teach me.

He walks out of the shadows from the side of the house and hops up the steps. "Hey, Squirt." He ruffles my hair and I jerk away. I don't want no boy cooties. Teane says they a pain to get rid of, and sometimes you can't get rid of them at all they so strong.

Wayne whistles past me and through the front door. I count to seven before he's back outside. Another hour 'til dinner. Nana doesn't like nobody bothering her in the kitchen when she cooks. Wayne's going to try and grab my hair again, but I'm ready this time. When his clunky feet hit the second step, I jerk my head to the right. He laughs and sits down on the steps with me.

"So what's up, Squirt?"

"Just you shut your mouth or I'm going to tell Nana on you." Wayne picks on me. He says it's what boys do to girls, but I never hear him messing with Teane. She's three years older than him and usually three times meaner. She doesn't waste her time with me unless she wants to make me feel stupid. She's real good at that.

"Little Donetta going to run to her big Nana?"

I stick my tongue out at Wayne's baby voice. I want to laugh and say I seen him run from Nana when she gets the belt out, but I don't want him to leave me alone. I can ignore Wayne's teasing because sometimes he'll play with me. Not like Teane. But I ain't never going to let him know that.

"So what are you doing out here on the porch? It's getting cool out." He nudges my shoulder with his knee and I push him back, but not too hard. "Nana won't be happy with you."

"So?" I shrug my shoulders, crossing my fingers in my head that Nana isn't listening or watching us. "Just waiting for dinner."

"You want to go play our game? We got time before dinner's ready."

I plant my feet on the ground. They're ready to run upstairs with Wayne, but I know I got to act bored. When he knows how much I want to play, he laughs and walks away. He tricks me like that. I shrug my shoulders again. "I guess." He doesn't say nothing. Maybe he's laughing at me, the little kid. He said before that he's too big to play with little kids.

"Let's go," he says and stands up. He walks back into the house, not waiting for me. I finally let my smile come out, just for a second as I jump up from the step, before sticking it way down deep inside me. I got to stay cool.

We always play doctor up in Momma's room. She don't stay with us no more, not since she left me at Nana's. Nana only comes up here on cleaning day, when she polishes the floors until they're like mirrors. Wayne says Nana shouldn't know we play up here. He says all the kids play doctor and Nana'd be furious if she found out I was playing too. I'm happy I got a secret, a secret like real friends, even if it has to be with Wayne.

He smooths his imaginary beard down his face, trying to look smart. He looks confused to me, but I don't tell him that. "Well, now, Miz Donetta." He likes to drag out names. "Let's see if we can find your problem here."

I sit on the big marshmallow bed and wait for the doctor to start. He tilts my chin up and looks in my eyes and mouth. He tells me to say "ahh" and I do, wondering how hard it'll be to get the boy cooties off. I hope my bath tonight'll take care of it. I got to remember to use lots of soap.

He picks up a rusty metal bottle cap and rolls it around his fingers. He leans in close and puts the cool metal to my chest, just above the edge of my cotton top. "Breathe in deeply."

I drag the breath from the bottom of my stomach and push it through my chest and out of my stomach, forcing it out for the doctor to look at. My head feels like a balloon bobbing on the afternoon wind. The balloon shakes, ready to pop, and I whoosh the air back inside, throwing my body forward. The doctor steps back.

"Sounds fine to me, Miz Donetta." He winks and picks up my arm, placing his fingers on my wrist. His other hand hangs to my knee and I try to remember every place he touches. "Yep, you sure are a healthy girl."

He scratches the short hairs on the back of his head, then picks up my arm and lets it drop again. He hits both of my knees and watches them jerk kick. He looks back at my head, turning it from side to side, looking in my ears.

Lots of soap tonight. Nana'll be proud of how clean I'll be.

"I ain't got much to do seeing as you're so healthy. I need a sick patient."

It's always the same story. Wayne's the doctor, but I ain't never sick enough for him. Not like my real doctors. So then I bring him a sick patient. I usually bring our neighbor because she's too fat to be healthy. "I can go get Cakey." Wayne likes playing doctor with her. He's got lots to examine.

He nods and smiles, and I jump off the bed and run through our pretend waiting room and down the stairs. I run all the way to the side of the porch and start yelling for Cakey in the house next door. Mrs. Scott sticks her head out the front door and I tell her we're playing and need Cakey. I almost tell her to hurry up, but Nana'd whip me good to talk like that to a grownup.

Cakey's real name's Catherine Ann, but everybody calls her Cakey. Except Nana. I figure she got her nickname because she likes to eat so much cake and sweets. The first time Nana brought me candy, I shared with Cakey, like a good Christian, and Nana was proud of me. I only got one piece of the candy. Since then, I hide when Nana brings me candy. Or I eat it all during the story telling.

Cakey comes out onto the neighboring porch, her body packed in a white dress that makes her skin look blacker than normal. "Cakey, we playing doctor and Wayne said to come get you."

"Hush, girl," Cakey says, frowning her huge rubbery lips. She looks back into the house and pulls the door shut. "Don't you know nothing, girl? That's our game. Don't go telling nobody we playing it."

She lumbers down her steps and over to our porch and I want to get behind her and push her to move her big body faster. Wayne might get bored and leave and then I'd be stuck with just Cakey, who treats me like a baby even though she's only thirteen. She finally gets up our steps and I bolt through the door ahead of her, running up the stairs to catch Wayne before he leaves.

I run through the waiting room and into Momma's room, where Wayne's on the bed, arms and legs sprawled, staring at the ceiling. He sits up when I rush in.

"She coming?"

I nod.

"Well, then, Miz Donetta, you need to get out into that waiting room. You don't want to catch nothing if she's sick." He gets off the bed and shoos me into the waiting room, a cubbyhole next to Momma's room.

Cakey finally heaves herself up the last step and Wayne escorts her into Momma's room, mumbling about her being so sick, she should have come sooner. He closes the door behind them and I say a silent prayer that I don't get sick, too. Nana doesn't give me no candy when I'm sick, just yucky old oatmeal.

I sit on the high-backed chair and wait, looking at the purple flowers on the wallpaper They're staring back at me from all sides and I see myself running though the soft petals. I look down at the shiny wooden floor that my feet barely touch, but there ain't nothing to see there except the spots where our feet wore on the polish. I think Cakey's feet've worn down the most polish.

Cakey's always in the doctor's office for a long time. She's always real sick.

The stairs squeak. Nana's coming—I have to hide. I hold my breath, trying to think of an excuse, wondering what Nana'll say and how can I get out of the trouble that I know is coming. But it's Teane's head with her thick dark braids poking around the corner. Teane is the prettiest girl I know, if you ignore her meanness. At least until she smiles.

"What you doing up here?" Her voice is soft and cool like sweet chunks of watermelon in the afternoon shade. But I know her sugary voice is just for pretend. I wait for the change. It shows up when I'm not looking, so I got to concentrate.

I smooth my thin skirt over my legs and plan what to say. "Playing." My knees jut into the fabric, like Nana's knees when she's telling me stories.

"Playing what?"

I force my hands to the edge of the chair and look up at Teane. "Doctor." I shrug. It's no big deal. All the kids play it.

She puts one hand on her hip and leans into the doorframe. "Wayne's in there." I nod, but she isn't asking. She bends down to me. "Cakey in there with him?" I nod again. One eyebrow floats up into a pretty arch above her molasses brown eyes.

"Doctor's listening to her heart." My legs are kicking back and forth under the chair. I can't help smiling. Wayne wants to play with me and now Teane's being nice to me. My smile wraps around to the backs of my ears. "Cakey' s always real sick." I try to be grown up about it, but I can't stop smiling.

Teane barks out a laugh and straightens in the doorway. She crosses her arms and I feel the teasing oozing out of her eyes. "Don't you know nothing?" She smiles like an angry dog, showing her perfect row of giant bucked teeth. Her head wiggles back and forth on her neck. "They doing it."

I bite my lip and study the polished floor. "Doing it" must be bad. *Please, God, don't let Teane tell Nana on me.* I peek up at Teane, wondering if God's answered my prayer.

"Wayne's in there sticking his thing into Cakey." She throws back her head with another bark.

"Nuh-uh!"

Just like Teane. She starts nice, but she's just playing with me. I should've known she wouldn't stay nice to me.

"He's playing doctor. He's just listening to her heart and stuff." I tell the purple flowers to take Teane away, but they don't help me none.

"How long it take Wayne to play with you?" I shrug and beg the flowers to help. "Now how long he been playing with Cakey?"

I watch her eyebrow arch again, but it isn't pretty no more. Now it's laughing at me and I want to rip it off and stomp it into the floor polish.

"Girl, they doing it. You know that hole you got between your legs? Yeah, down there." She points to my private area, that place my eyes can't stay away from while Teane talks, and my face burns. No wonder she teases me, as stupid as I am, and the burn spreads to my ears and neck. "Wayne's putting his little pee-pee in Cakey's hole right now."

My eyelashes fan up and down and I'm not sure if they're trying to cool my face or stop the tears. "Don't you tease me. I'm going to tell Nana." My legs are kicking again and if she moves just a little to my left I can kick her down the stairs.

She takes two steps, pulls me off the chair with one arm and sweeps the door open with the other. She throws me around and there I stand in front of the marshmallow bed with Wayne's naked bottom up in the air over Cakey's black rolls.

Nana would whoop me if she saw me in here. I shouldn't be looking at Wayne's backside, but he's playing a new doctor with Cakey. Wayne rolls off Cakey and grabs his shorts, but I see his thing anyway and now I know Nana will be coming through the door. Cakey's dress is pulled up to her stomach and she ain't wearing no underwear and I don't think this is a game I want to play. Teane laughs and I don't know why she isn't afraid of Nana finding us. I need to run away, run downstairs and wait for dinner, but if I move, maybe Nana will hear my footsteps and come to see what's going on and then how could I explain to her so she won't be mad? She'll send me to bed and never tell me another story and it's all Wayne's fault because he tricked me like he tricks everyone.

Stupid Wayne and mean Teane and now Cakey's playing along, even though she's just as afraid of Nana. Teane's still laughing and I want to tell her to shut up but I know she'll slap me if I do. I have to block out the laughing. I stomp out the door and through the waiting room. I don't care if Nana comes and sees me now. She'll make Teane stop laughing. Nobody laughs when Nana's angry. I stomp down the stairs, making my footsteps louder and louder, but they're never loud enough.

I get to the bottom of the stairs and Nana's there, wiping her hands on her apron and watching me stomp. She's not happy. I'm bothering her with my noise. I look down to the floor, but I don't care if she punishes me. She can send me to my room and I won't have to listen to Teane's laughing or look at Wayne's tricking face no more. Nana doesn't talk. She takes my hand and leads me back to the kitchen, sets me squarely on a stool next to the wall, and pretends not to see me wiping away my stupid tears.

***

I don't play doctor no more. Wayne never asks me to, but I wouldn't anyway. I never got in trouble, so I don't think they told anyone what we were doing, but I don't want to risk it no more. And I don't like Wayne tricking me. Cakey doesn't come over, but I think it's because her momma's mad at her for getting so fat. She doesn't even fit into her own clothes anymore. If she could put some of that fat onto my legs, then I bet her momma would be happy. I sure would.

I can hear her momma yelling at her from my place on the porch. I hear the screeching and I move to the bottom step and lean over my knees, cross my arms around my legs, and smile because something's finally blocked out Teane's laughter. Teane must have put a spell on me because her laughter chases me everywhere, even into the Special Room when Nana tells her stories, although it's not as loud in there. But I can't hear the laughter with all that screeching next door.

It sounds like Cakey. Her momma must be deaf, it's so loud. I sink my head farther into my chest and let the screams push out the laughter and wonder why her momma's beating her so hard this time. The screams get louder and I feel them go in my ears, through my head, down my back where they turn around and return to my head. They're chasing Teane's laughter and I feel the fight going on in my head, a white explosion when they meet. I squeeze my eyes shut, but the explosions continue and I don't want this fight anymore.

I jump up and run into the house, trying to hide from all the screams and laughter, sneaking into the Special Room. I slide into the corner behind Nana's chair and lay down on the cool floor, pressing my cheek against smooth wood and hiding in the waxy smell of the polish. I breathe in deeply and focus on the smell. Soon I'm dreaming of purple flowers, some of them screaming at me and others laughing.

I feel a movement in the floor and open my eyes. Someone's turned on the lights, but I'm still hidden by the shadow of Granddaddy's chair. I hold my breath and try not to move. Nana'll be super mad if I'm in here alone. I see Nana's feet shuffle into the room and the chair in front of me move with her weight. A pair of shiny black leather shoes clicks in after her, chipping away the polished floor. The shoes click over to the sofa in front of Nana and sit down with a loud *hurumph*.

"This ain't just my problem." Cakey's momma's voice is squeaky, like I imagine a mouse's to be, if a mouse could talk. "I raised my girl right."

"Catherine Ann is a smart girl." Nana measures out each of her words, the way she does when she knows she's right but the person she's talking to hasn't figured it out yet.

"It's the work of the devil." *Squeak, squeak.* "That boy ain't no good and I told you that the day his daddy left him here. You should've made his daddy take him, let him beat some more sense into him."

"What would you like me to do about this situation?" The chair in front of me shifts slightly and I push back into the corner. *Please, God, don't let her see me back here.*

"His daddy would put a hand to him, that's what he'd do."

Nana sighs and stands up, her feet turning to the door. "Let me find Wayne." She walks out of the door, but Mrs. Scott continues talking to herself about letting Wayne's daddy take care of everything.

I try not to laugh because Wayne really got caught doing something bad if Nana's thinking to call his daddy. Wayne's afraid of Nana just as much as the rest of us, but he's terrified of his daddy.

I wonder if I can slip out of the room before Nana returns. I peek around the corner of the chair. Mrs. Scott's sitting on the long yellow couch that nobody ever sits on, making faces at something in her arms. She's mumbling and smiling at it, and then telling it loudly that Wayne'll get what he deserves. I don't think she'll see me if I shimmy out along the floor, but I want to hear what kind of trouble Wayne's in so I can laugh at him.

I start to ease back behind the chair when I see a tiny arm pop out of the bundle of cloth Mrs. Scott's talking to. She fusses over the baby, wrapping and rewrapping the material around the arm, still mumbling about Wayne.

Nana returns, Wayne tripping behind her, and I wish I could stick out my tongue at him and laugh. Nana sits back in her chair, but Wayne keeps standing, looking around the room, studying everything except Mrs. Scott and the baby.

"Wayne, it seems you and Catherine Ann have a situation to deal with," Nana says.

He shrugs and looks around the room some more. I see Teane crawling down the hall. She stops just out of Nana's view and leans back against the wall, looks at me, and mouths the word "doctor" before smiling her bucked teeth smile.

"What do you want to do about it?" Nana's voice reminds me there are others in the room.

Wayne's in trouble for playing doctor, which means I'm in trouble too, and I suck in my bottom lip. I don't want to cry, I don't want Teane to see me or Nana to hear me, but I don't think I can stop it.

"There ain't no want about it," Mrs. Scott says, and the baby starts crying. "There, see there? That's your problem, boy. That's what you gots to deal with now. He's your baby, too."

Wayne bows his head and scowls at the floor. Teane's mouthing the word "doctor" again and rocking a pretend baby in her arms. Mrs. Scott's still yelling at Wayne, but all I can think is that Nana's going to be angry with me. She might even send me away, back to Momma. I don't remember Wayne ever touching my stomach or saying strange words to me, but he's good at tricking people. I don't feel like I should have a baby. Teane says I don't know nothing anyway, so maybe I wouldn't even know it.

"Let me see that baby." The crying quiets to Nana's shushes.

Nana won't tell me no more stories, she'll only tell them to my baby, and I can't stop my sniffling. I hate Wayne and his stupid tricks and him getting me in trouble when all I wanted was to play and now I got to have a baby because of him.

"There's no need to upset the baby. Let's listen to what Wayne has to say."

But Wayne doesn't say nothing, just rocks back and forth on his feet.

I'm surprised Nana's staying so calm instead of going for the belt. If I had the belt, I'd whip Wayne until his backside was purple. Him and his purple bottom on top of Cakey's black rolls and maybe they'd both get whooped together. I can see them back on Momma's bed with Nana standing over them with the belt. But that was the other doctor game, the one Wayne never played with me.

"Since Wayne seems to be at a loss for words, let me offer a solution." Nana's voice slices through the silence. "Wayne will go to work with his father and bring his pay to Catherine Ann every Sunday for the baby's needs. Will that be sufficient?"

Wayne looks like for sure he's going to crumple in a heap on the floor. Teane always says their daddy likes to give Wayne bruises for no reason. I want to laugh at Wayne, getting in trouble for playing doctor and tricking me.

"It'll do," Mrs. Scott says. "For now." The couch sighs as she stands up and collects the baby from Nana. She walks past Wayne and out the door, ignoring Teane, who isn't smiling no more.

She understands just like me. Wayne's in big trouble, the biggest, too big for the belt.

"Wayne, go pack your things and we'll get you to your father's tomorrow," Nana says.

Wayne shuffles out of the room, kicking Teane as he walks by. Teane cries out, then bites her lip and jumps up before Nana can say something. I laugh and stick my tongue out at her.

"Donetta?"

My stomach drops to the floor. I've given myself away.

I crawl out from behind the chair. I can't hide from her now. I sit on the floor in front of her, tugging my skirt down. I squeeze my eyes shut, but the tears come anyway. She's not saying nothing, but my face is burning from her stare.

"Do I have to go away, too?" I don't want to hear her answer, but I got to know.

She laughs a little, but it sounds like it got caught in her throat on the way up. "You are going to stay right here and listen to a story."

"Am I going to have a baby?" I try to look up to her, but I can only get as high as the piece of lint on her gray skirt. "Me and Wayne, I just wanted to play, but I think he tricked me too."

She's going to take me upstairs for the belt before she sends me away, but I hope it's not to Momma's room. I don't want to go there no more. I don't want to see the marshmallow bed and Cakey's rolls and Wayne's thing.

"Donetta, you haven't done anything wrong." Her voice is like the sugar candy. I look up and she is smiling. "Wayne and Cakey did something very different, something they aren't grown up enough for. You were just playing."

She smiles and I think of the other game, the doctor game for the really sick people, and what Teane said about what they was doing behind the closed door.

"Would you like me to tell you the story about the bad baby boy?"

I shake my head. She tries to smile, but it's the same fake smile she gave Momma the day she left me with Nana. I know we've just shared a secret, a grownup secret, and Nana's stories don't seem real no more.

A PURPOSEFUL WALK

Carlos discovered his sanity under a pile of shoes in the back of his grandmother's closet. He didn't remember leaving it there, under the dusty Oxfords and light-colored sandals of his grandmother's youth, but he figured he had unknowingly dropped it one day and his grandmother had picked it up during one of her cleaning sprints. He plucked it from the shoes, deposited it in his coat pocket, then continued to scrounge around for the matching fuzzy slipper that his grandmother had sent him to find before the bridge party started in the facility's common area.

"Mee-maw?" he called out to her. "No slippers."

"Well of course not! They're on my feet, silly," she said from behind him. "Why are you digging around in my closet?"

Carlos turned to see his grandmother showing off two feet wrapped in plush gray slippers. Like Vanna White pointing to a new puzzle. He rolled his eyes and stood up. "What else, Mee-maw?"

"Just skeedaddle," she said. "I got me some butt to whoop. That Mr. Jenkins, he's going down today."

"Alright, young lady, you have fun out there." He hugged her, careful not to put too much pressure on her brittle bones. "And don't worry, I've got the bail money set aside for you." He winked at their shared joke and was out the door, striding purposefully through the sterile halls, head down, eyes averted. Making eye contact with any of the residents in the old age home always led to endless stories of how he reminded someone of so-and-so back in the day. Carlos didn't have time for stories today. He didn't have time for any delays.

He shoved his hands in his pockets and remembered his sanity. His left hand closed around it, the clamminess of his hand making his sanity feel slick and cool. He turned down a hall that led past the common area to the facility's front entrance. He pulled up short when he saw the unexpected crowd of people. So many old eyes to escape.

"Head down, eyes averted, purposeful walk," he mumbled to himself, focusing on the large grayish floor tiles flecked with orange and yellow and white. He focused on each foot as it shuffled forward in its turn. "Head down, eyes averted, purposeful walk." He refused to be sucked into the sea of people milling about. "Head down, eyes averted, purposeful walk." How many more steps until the door to his escape?

"Carlos, my boy." Mr. Jenkins called out to him through the crowd.

Carlos tightened his grip on his sanity, the sweat from his palm now making it too slippery to hold on to. Carlos dropped his head lower, raised his right hand to wave, and remained focused on the floor in front of him. "No—no—sorry, Mr. J. No time today. Games to play. On my way."

Several old ladies appeared in front of Carlos, and he jerked his hips and shoulders back to avoid touching them while his feet continued to carry him closer to the front door. "So close, so close," he said. "3...2...1..."

He broke through the front doors and stepped out into the bright sunshine, lifting his arms in victory above his head but still not looking up as he inhaled the crisp March air. A small knot of people were moving toward him, toward the door. He had to get past them before they trapped him on the steps.

He lowered his arms, dropping his right arm to be perpendicular to his body while his left hand returned to clasp his sanity. "Make way, coming through," he said over the chattering emerging from the group. He tightened his right hand into a fist, then lunged forward. "Coming through!" he said, his agitation raising his voice by several decibels. He pushed his way down the steps, through the middle of the crowd, and away from their angry stares and sarcastic excuse-mes.

He shrugged as he moved along the sidewalk. He had warned them. *No need to get snippy about it.*

"No need!" he yelled back over his shoulder, still not making eye contact with anyone. "No need at all!"

He shrugged his coat up higher around his neck, protecting himself from the cold pollution of the city streets. "People!" he huffed in a white cloud of warm breath, then sidestepped to avoid his breath from coming back into his face. He couldn't understand people these days. Didn't they know that not everyone has time to just sit around listening to boring stories or talking about the weather and their aching bones? He couldn't be late. Not today. "People," he said to the passers-by. "People, people, people—not today!"

"Head down, eyes averted, purposeful walk," he mumbled, moving further along the sidewalk. He knew the route by heart, knew when to swerve to avoid the broken cement, when to hunch up his shoulders so the people sitting at the windows in the cafe wouldn't distract him, when to run to make the next crosswalk signal, and when to slow down to avoid the crowds exiting the subway. He had spent weeks figuring out the best times to visit his grandmother while avoiding all the distractions on the streets. Mee-maw called them loons. The loons were wasteful—wasteful with their time and their money and their lives—and Carlos hated wastefulness. He was all about economy. Like planning his routes. Planning created economy. It saved his time and prevented frustration.

A small boy stood in his path, and Carlos stopped midstep, unsure which way to go. He grunted at the boy, who looked up at Carlos and giggled.

Planning was supposed to prevent frustration, but it didn't always work. Now Carlos was faced with a decision, and he didn't like decisions. If he moved left around the boy, he would run into more people as they moved along the sidewalk. If he moved right, he would be closer to the curb, and Carlos didn't like the curb. Too much unpredictability, with people getting in and out of cabs or crossing the street where they shouldn't be. And the trash cans, placed willy-nilly at odd intervals. No, the city was just as much a wasteful loon as the people living inside it. Carlos jammed his hands into his pockets and stared at the little boy, who looked back at Carlos, giggling again.

"Economy, people," Carlos whispered as he stroked his sanity, its cool surface smooth and distraction-free.

The boy clapped several times, then spun around in a circle, keeping his face turned up to Carlos. He stopped, facing Carlos, his head still echoing the spinning, then giggled again. He stared at Carlos, waiting.

"No time today," Carlos mumbled.

The boy giggled again. He clapped his hands once more, then pointed at Carlos, giggling.

Carlos's fingers froze on his sanity. The boy clapped again, then pointed at Carlos. This time, no giggles.

"On my way," Carlos whispered.

The boy grabbed Carlos's coat sleeve and tugged on it until Carlos pulled his hand from his pocket. The boy grabbed his hand and ran in a circle around Carlos, dragging him along so that the older man was forced to spin in a circle, much like the boy had done. Carlos wanted to yell "wasteful, wasteful loon." He wanted to tell the boy to stop, to get out of his way because he can't be delayed, not today.

But the boy giggled again.

Carlos lifted his head to keep his balance as the boy spun him around and around. Carlos saw the store fronts and sidewalk and taxis and commuters and towering gray buildings and stairs diving underground all spinning around him again and again and again, becoming a soupy mess of grays and exhaust fumes and thundering footsteps. And through it all, he heard the tinkling giggling, a sweet melody that punctuated every note in the soupy mess, as if highlighting its significance. Carlos breathed in the polluted smells and soaked up the chattering people and horn bursts and stretched out his arms as he spun round and round and round.

He smiled. "Fuck economy!" he gasped, his voice deep with orgasmic release.

The little boy ripped his hand from Carlos, who jerked to a stop. He opened his eyes and saw a woman wearing a dark blue suit and strict eyeliner grabbing at the little boy.

"Bobby, what did I tell you about talking to strangers!" She pulled the boy away from Carlos and down the sidewalk. Carlos turned to watch them walk away, staring after them until they crossed the intersection and disappeared into the masses. Carlos watched and waited, but Bobby never turned back to say goodbye.

Carlos shuffled around and went on his way, once again following his planned pathway to avoid distractions and wasteful loons. He grasped for his sanity, but it no longer provided the cool reassurance he was seeking. Instead, he felt in it the icy cold of death.

He veered off his planned path, stumbled to the nearest trash can, and tossed his sanity deep within the city's refuse. "Fuck economy," he said once again, then glanced up and down the sidewalk.

He didn't know where to go, which path to follow. He didn't even see a path through the crowds of people marching along the sidewalks. For the first time, Carlos giggled.

WHAT WOULD JERRY DO?

Sam focused on the TV, trying to ignore Aunt Sarah. Since Josey had walked out almost three weeks ago, Aunt Sarah had driven the sixty-two miles from Birmingham to Lawley every third day after her bingo game to wash the dishes and sweep out the one-room cabin while tsk-tsking at Sam as he sat on the cracked leather couch, watching the junkyard black-and-white TV. Aunt Sarah was already drying the dishes. She would be leaving soon, but Sam could still hear her tsk-tsk around her mumbles. She wouldn't talk too loudly now. The baby was sleeping in her crib in the corner, and Aunt Sarah would be afraid of waking her.

Sam tried to readjust, but he stuck to the fake leather. He sighed and slumped back into his original position, legs sprawled, head propped on one hand, his other hand stuck between the cushions. Jerry Springer was on TV. Aunt Sarah hated Jerry, said he was the Devil himself trying to convert even more heathens. Sam believed that Jerry was the only man alive who saw the world for what it truly was. Jerry listened. He listened no matter what sin had been committed. Sam knew Jerry'd be a good friend.

Today's show: teenage girls who seduced their fathers. Sam chuckled. Jerry was right on today. Aunt Sarah would drop the dishes in her rush to cross herself a thousand times while escaping the Devil's handiwork. He heard the wooden floor scream as Aunt Sarah shifted and turned to look at the TV. She rolled her eyes and huffed.

"Don't you worry none," she said, drying the enamel off the chipped plate, trying to talk over the Devil. "That wife of yours, she just a child. She scared now, but she gonna come to her senses. She's a momma now. Your Aunt Sarah—she knows." She turned back to the sink. "She be back for Sunday. Your momma done come to me in my dreams and told me so. Said she's gonna see her own grandbaby baptized in a sweet honey pool."

Over the last thirty years Aunt Sarah had been visited by her sister so many times that Sam had lost count. Sam hadn't seen her since that night she drove off to work and ended up in the cemetery. She never visited his dreams.

Sam peeled himself off the couch and turned up the volume. The audience gasped and booed and the censors bleeped all the nasty words, but Sam knew what they were saying, knew Jerry'd be listening with his concerned look. Aunt Sarah grumbled over to the TV.

"Don't you be waking that baby." Her husky whisper drowned out the audience. "I done got her to sleep, no thanks to your lazy butt. Reverend Joe says she needs to be rested, so you let her sleep."

Sam stuck his hand back between the cushions.

"You'd better go find your wife, decide on a name for that child. That's what a husband's supposed to do, not sit around watching heathens."

Aunt Sarah dried her hands, and Sam listened to her straighten the few dishes on the counter. She thundered across the wooden floor, stopping in the corner for one last look at the baby before the drive home. "I'll be telling your Mom-mom and Poppy all about you soon, little angel." Sam held his breath. Aunt Sarah's only daughter had gotten lost walking home from school before Sam and Josey got married. A group of teenage boys in a big blue Ford had found her. Aunt Sarah's husband walked in their bathroom and shot himself in the heart the day they got the call. Aunt Sarah found the body, and the next Sunday she found God.

But Sam never found God. He never really looked. He found Josey, who quit school because she wanted to play house and Sam liked pretending that he made her happy, that she needed him. Not that he was such a bad man. He had a job at the Lawley garage and he preferred just to let people be. Aunt Sarah had said he was getting close to forty, which meant he needed to get his family started before it was too late. She didn't listen, just talked. Sam just wanted Aunt Sarah to shut up. Having a sleeping baby helped.

Aunt Sarah opened the door to the cabin and pulled the keys to her old Thunderbird out of her purse. "Don't you worry, she'll be back. And I'll see ya'll Sunday morning."

The audience chanted *Jerry–Jerry*. Sam didn't start breathing again until the sound of her car faded down the half-mile gravel lane that led to the highway that led to Lawley and Birmingham and the real world.

Josey wasn't coming home. He would let Aunt Sarah stay in her own God-fearing world, he would never show her the letter. He pulled his hand out from between the cushions and brought the letter up to the light of the TV. When he had first found it under the baby's plastic panties and behind the bottle of stale baby powder, it still had the smell of Josey's dollar store lavender soap. Now it smelled like his sweat. He had been looking for the extra food stamps he knew Josey took to pay for her strawberry milk. She thought she was smarter than Sam, that he didn't now she bought food for herself instead of her family He just let her be, let her live her life, sins and all, like Jerry'd do.

He opened the folder letter and looked down at the slow, bold writing. It wasn't Josey's writing. He didn't know who had written it, but he didn't think that was important. What was important was that Josey had liked to walk up and down the lane at night. She had insisted on walking alone, she needed the break from the baby, from him. Every night she had walked up and down the lane, her second-hand tennis shoes crunching in the gravel past the small pond and mosquitoes and the honeysuckle bushes, and one night she hadn't come back.

He studied the letter, looking for something he had missed, some hidden word or unseen clue, but he had the message memorized. Nothing new this time.

Josey girl, you're making me crazy, and I can't stand it no more. Whatever you need, just let me have you, just once. I'll be there, by the honeysuckle and I'll wait all night if I have to. But I'll be ready for you.

The audience applauded at the next guest. They wouldn't applaud Josey. They would boo her for abandoning her husband. They would sympathize with Sam, the poor husband who stood by her side. But the audience was fickle. They changed sides, and as Josey explained, they would convert to her following. He wasn't a perfect husband. He didn't even know what a husband was exactly. Maybe he didn't do the job correctly. He should've worked more at the garage, gotten more money. He should've taken the extra food stamps from Josey. He should've asked her why she walked the lane alone while he sat inside watching TV and the baby slept. He should've told Aunt Sarah to leave her alone, to quit preaching, to stop cleaning and let Josey be the woman of the house. And Jerry would hear him and convince Josey to give him another chance, to let him be a husband, a father, maybe even a friend.

The baby shuffled and whined. She never cried. She would whimper and grunt, but she didn't cry. Sometimes he found her lying in the crib, looking at nothing, waiting.

That's when he felt closest to her, like she actually could be of his own blood. She whined again and he walked to the corner, wiping the sweat from the backs of his legs. She looked at him and grunted. He hefted her out of the crib and bounced around the room with her. She didn't make any noise.

He went outside, walked down the lane and stood bouncing the baby and looking up and down the highway. A new car sped by and the baby jerked. But she didn't cry. He followed the taillights of the car down the road as it zoomed to Lawley. Josey could be in a car like that, a nice smooth car that flowed down the roads of the county. She could be driving around and enjoying her new life, forgetting Sam and the baby and the gravel lane to the one-room cabin. He turned and walked back to his house.

He passed the honeysuckle shrubs and was surrounded by the sweet smell. His stomach lurched at the smell and he stopped. The baby whined, but he didn't bounce her. He walked behind the honeysuckle bush, to the space where they must have met, every night, and heaved up the hot dog and chips he had eaten before Aunt Sarah came. He spit several times and the baby watched. He tried to get the bitter taste off his tongue. He spit out and breathed in the sweet honeysuckle smell that must have encircled them as they sat here, kissing and groping and laughing at Sam and Jerry and the baby. Josey would laugh the loudest and her man would try to hush her, afraid of Sam just a few steps away. But she would swat at him. She wasn't afraid of Sam. Sam swatted at the cloud of mosquitoes and the baby whined and grunted. He held her tighter and walked to the edge of the small pond. He sat in the water to cool off, setting the baby in front of him in the water. She grunted once and then calmed down.

Josey would find them here and cry, like she always did when she saw Sam with the baby. She would cry and scream and grab the baby and run into the house. Josey didn't like the pond. In the summer, it was full of snakes and Josey was terrified of snakes. But she wouldn't come back this time, not in the daylight, not when he could see her. She would sneak into the single room at night, when the moon was full and she would be able to see the snakes sliding over the ground and run around them. She would barely open the door, just enough to squeak in and cower across the floor barefoot. She wouldn't check on the baby, wouldn't even walk near the crib. She would tiptoe straight to the old wicker dresser, confident she wouldn't wake Sam and afraid of the baby. And she'd reach under the plastic panties, behind the stale baby powder and slide out the food stamps and love letter while Sam watched from the bed. He wouldn't stop her. He wouldn't yell or scream or beg her to stay. But he'd wait to see if just once as she slinked back to her secret lover she'd hesitate.

She wouldn't.

Jerry would reassure Sam, put his hand on Sam's shoulder, ask Josey why she did such a horrible thing to such a nice man. Josey had been trouble from that first Friday night, when she brought in her mama's car to the garage and screamed and yelled and cried for him to fix the long scratch on the side. He had tried to calm her down, explain it wasn't something to be fixed in a few minutes. She'd thrown herself into his chest, screaming her mama would beat her to death this time, and Sam had just done what came natural. He hadn't asked her age, hadn't even thought about it, until three weeks later when she showed up at the garage again and said she had enough proof growing in her to put him away for sleeping with a fifteen-year-old unless he took care of her. So they got married and Aunt Sarah was happy and Josey was happy and Sam was satisfied that they would be happy and leave him alone with Jerry, But then the baby had been born and the walks had started, Josey alone up and down the gravel drive, past the pond and the honeysuckle.

Sam scooted down further into the pond and the baby slid into the mud and water, away from the mosquitoes and snakes and honeysuckle and Sam. She didn't whine. She looked up at Sam and smiled. She understood. Jerry would too. Aunt Sarah would be angry she missed the private baptism. He didn't know what to say. He knew there must be some special words, a prayer or chant, but Aunt Sarah's God would just have to make do. Jerry would know what to say, but the TV wouldn't reach out this far. He pulled the letter out of his pocket. He dropped it into the water and let it float around where the baby used to be, where tiny air bubbles bounced to the top of the water. He watched the bubbles bounce and pop until there weren't anymore, then stood up and shook water off his legs. He walked past the honeysuckle back to the highway and waited for another car to pass. Eventually someone would stop and give him a ride. He had figured it out once that it would take two days to drive to Chicago, almost two months to walk. He hoped the audience would applaud for him But at least he and Jerry could talk about how the world truly was. At least Jerry would listen.

THE STONE

Kennedy looked out over the lake and across the string of concrete that connected Two Lakes to the rest of the world. The bridge crossed over the lake and onto Highway 201 and who knew where that led, but Kennedy was determined to find out. He wanted to follow that highway to his escape.

"C'mon, you guys," Harold whined. "Let's go back to my house. My mom said she was going to make a cherry pie today."

Kennedy frowned. Harold's chubby cheeks looked paler than usual, despite the pink flush from the hot sun. He was technically the oldest of the three soon-to-be fifth graders, but his whining and his prominent baby fat made him seem like the youngest. He also seemed to have a knack for interrupting Kennedy's daydreams of escape.

"Harold, don't be such a wimp. Just take it easy," Tom said, scratching his lightly freckled stomach while looking out over the lake. "We're just looking. It's not like we're gonna do anything."

"What are we doing out here anyway?" Harold said, his voice becoming tinny.

Kennedy shrugged. "Nothing. No worries." He hoped that was the truth.

"Yeah, well my parents are gonna be pissed if they find out we were out here. Did you hear about Johnny Sampson?" Harold nodded toward the water. "Nearly drowned. Said something pulled him under."

They were at the larger of the two lakes, the one that had been closed to swimming since the Army Corps of Engineers built it in the early 1940s.

"Dumbass," Tom said. "There's nothing pulling him under except his own stupidity."

Kennedy sighed. Tom thought everyone was stupid. Kennedy wanted to point out that Tom had barely passed fourth grade. And third grade. Kennedy thought that the teachers were afraid of Tom's dad, which is why they kept passing Tom.

"Yeah, but it's not just Johnny," Harold said. "His brother and his brother's girlfriend saw it too."

"Saw what exactly?" Kennedy asked.

Harold glanced at the lake, then moved closer to Kennedy. "It had long tentacles and glowing eyes."

Tom laughed.

Harold hushed him, nervously watching the water. "Don't wake it up," he hissed through clenched teeth.

Tom laughed louder.

Kennedy forced a smile for Harold, trying to reassure him, but Harold turned his back to the other two boys. He moved up the beach to throw stones at the back of the No Swimming sign, the ping of the stones vibrating in Kennedy's ears, making goose bumps scurry up the nape of his neck. He ground his teeth and moved to stand next to Tom.

"They say it's haunted," Kennedy said.

Tom snorted. "Haunted I could buy. Hell, my daddy said his crazy old aunt refused to leave."

"Seriously?" Kennedy looked out over the dark blue water. "She'd be a bitch of a ghost. Even my daddy'd be scared of her." Tom raised an eyebrow. "She's probably out there right now, swimming around that old church."

Kennedy smiled, trying to ignore the shiver along his spine. He didn't believe the stories that people refused to leave their homes before the engineers flooded the valley. Kennedy's dad had been one of the hundreds of engineers to work on the project, and he couldn't imagine his father being so heartless to let people die like that.

Kennedy squinted against the sun reflecting off the surface of the lake. The mammoth church had stood taller than anything else in the community. The summer drought had dropped the water levels so low that he could see the cross from the top of the church standing out above the lake, reminding residents of Two Lakes of the sleeping community below the surface.

"We're gonna do something that nobody never done before," Tom said, almost to himself. He didn't take his eyes off the lake.

Kennedy looked at him, holding his breath, knowing trouble was imminent.

"Just imagine what everyone else would say. We'd be the greatest kids this town ever saw." Tom turned to Kennedy and locked eyes. "We'd be better than anybody else here."

Kennedy looked away first. "What are you talking about?"

Tom nodded at the cross. "Swimming out there."

Kennedy tried to remember the signs of sunstroke. Delusions had to be one warning sign. "Are you serious?" Kennedy finally said. "It's probably a mile out there, more even. You've never swum that far. And you know you couldn't, either." Kennedy laughed.

"Yeah, you're probably right." Tom shrugged. "I'm not a very good swimmer anyway."

He was silent for a minute, and Kennedy let go of the breath he had been holding. He was relieved there would be no adventure today. A little disappointed, but mostly relieved.

"Then again," Tom said, scratching at his blond buzz cut, "you always were a stronger swimmer than anybody. Hell, I bet you're the strongest swimmer in the whole county."

Kennedy let the challenge hang in the air, refusing to take the bait. He focused on the *ping ping* of Harold's stones and the smell of wet sand at his feet. Anything but Tom.

"You could easily swim out there, have a look around that cross, and then come back and tell us all what it's like," Tom said, shielding his eyes against the sun.

Kennedy rolled his eyes.

"Man," Tom said, "ain't nobody ever done that, not even that asshole Dennis. You'd be able to do something that he's too chickenshit to do."

Kennedy's knees felt weak just thinking about Dennis— not because the seventh grader bullied him, but because he was a daily reminder that Kennedy's father had left because of his feeble little coward of a boy. Kennedy bristled at his own spinelessness. He imagined how empowering it would be to gloat over Dennis. He would act all innocent when he asked Dennis about the last time he had braved the haunted waters. And he would pat Dennis on the shoulder when he bowed his head, mumbling "never."

Kennedy looked at the cross once again. It wasn't really that far out there.

Tom nudged Kennedy's arm. "Man, Kennedy, if you could do this for us, me and Harold would owe you big time, right Harold?" Harold answered with a loud ping of a stone. Tom leaned closer. "I'd owe you big time."

Kennedy licked his lips, tasting a new, unexpected power. The idea of besting Dennis was nice, but having Tom look up to him? Kennedy brushed his dark hair back from his face. If he swam really fast, nothing under the surface would be able to come up and grab him, sucking him under the surface. Not that he believed in ghosts or monsters.

"Yeah," he said, nodding his head. "Yeah, I can do that."

The pings stopped and Kennedy felt Harold's stare. He kicked off his shoes and threw off his tank top. He walked knee-deep into the water, took a deep breath, smiled, and dove into the cool liquid. He pushed arm over arm, the way his mom had taught him, and kicked fiercely, daring something to try and stop him. He pushed and breathed, pushed and breathed, envisioning the cross growing larger before him, ignoring the shadows of sea monsters hiding in the corners of his mind.

Push, push, breathe. Push, push, breathe. A picture of the vacant town, cocooned in its watery grave beneath him came unbidden to his mind. He forced the picture from his thoughts. *Push harder, breathe deeper.*

A large shadow loomed in front of him, rising from the darkness of the lake's depths, reaching its slimy tentacles up to become entangled in Kennedy's legs, wrapping around his ankles to drag him down. Dennis laughed in his head. Kennedy bit his lip, telling his uncooperative legs to behave before he was sucked down and his lungs exploded out of his body. If he drowned, his mom would be pissed and his dad would be too ashamed to ever return.

He turned his head, lifting his face from the water and took a quick gulp of air. As the air rushed into his lungs, he turned back to the water. Relief washed over him as he realized the shadow was the steeple of the church.

He pulled himself up to the cross and thanked God for letting all the monsters sleep today. Just in case there were monsters. He looked up the cross towering above him. It was as big around as his waist and not so shiny here up close to it, but more of a dirty charcoal color. He pulled himself up and stood on one of the arms of the cross, hugging the center with his right arm. His feet tried to grip the cold metal. He wiped the water from his eyes, careful to keep his weight evenly distributed.

When he looked back to the shore, Tom was whooping it up, dancing around Harold on the sand, laughing and hollering. Kennedy couldn't make out the words, but he guessed Tom was already figuring out a way to broadcast this event to all the other kids in Two Lakes. Kennedy stood up taller, looking around the lake, feeling the conqueror deep inside him.

A breeze carried snippets of the voices from the shore to him. His skin broke out into goose bumps, and he tried to rub them away without losing his balance. He looked down at the dark water lapping at his feet and saw the dingy cross connect to a hazy steeple disappearing into clouded water. He wondered what else slept beneath the surface, what else he could conquer.

Tom and Harold waved at him from the shore. He heard the water splashing at his feet, a siren song luring him back into its seductive grip. The hair on the back of his neck stood on end. He told himself it was from his skin losing heat, but he knew it was lie. The water lapping at his feet was snickering at him now, telling him he was trapped. It whispered that the monsters were real, and they weren't sleeping anymore.

Kennedy considered staying on the cross until the others could go for help, maybe find a boat to come to his rescue. The whole town would come out to see how he got stranded on the cross in the middle of the lake. They would laugh at him and remind him of it every chance they got. His mom would beat him until he couldn't sit down and then take him to church to pray for forgiveness for his sins. Tom would be too embarrassed to be his friend. He would turn his back on him, maybe even become friends with Dennis instead, and they would both torment Kennedy. His eyes burned as he fought back tears. He wouldn't cry. He couldn't cry. He looked at Tom waving his arms. It was his stupid idea to swim out here. He had talked Kennedy into yet another mess, tricked him into a predicament where Kennedy was left to face the music. Or in this case, the monsters.

He looked at the water, heaved his chest, and decided he would make it back or drown trying. He wasn't going to wait on the cross for everybody to laugh at him. He closed his eyes, said a silent prayer promising not to fall for any of Tom's escapades if he just survived this last one, then dove in.

He tried not to think about what was at the bottom of the lake and hoped that it was sleeping too soundly to hear one tiny little boy splashing around on the surface. He pushed his arms over his head, but his muscles were already burning and he felt the beginnings of a cramp in his right side.

Something slithered past his leg, brushing the hairs and making him jerk wildly. He panicked and inhaled water, coughing and choking and sputtering. He wasn't going to make it. He would sink to the bottom of the lake and then wait for other foolish children to try to reach the cross before he rose and pulled them down to wait with him. He hoped his father at least made it back for the funeral. He squeezed his eyes shut, not wanting to see the monsters as they pulled him to his grave.

He felt a clammy grip on his arms just before he was ripped through the water, his nose and eyes filled with sand. *No, dammit.* His father would not be ashamed of him anymore. Kennedy tore at his face, trying to clear his vision and face his nightmare in his final moments.

He blinked and looked up to see Tom and Harold, smiling and chattering away. He couldn't understand what they were saying, but their faces burned red with excitement. His chest heaved with his labored breathing, and his knees burrowed into the sand as the sounds finally penetrated to his brain.

"Holy shit that was so cool!"

"What was out there?"

"I can't believe you did it."

"Is it really made of solid gold?"

"Way to go, Kennedy!"

Kennedy dragged himself out of the water His legs and arms were shaking as he trudged through the knee-deep water. Only once he was out of the water did he glance back at the cross and realize he was truly safe. He took several more heavy steps, waving Tom and Harold off before collapsing onto the sandy beach.

He rolled onto his back, closed his eyes, and let the warmth of the sand below him and the sun above him envelop him. He tried to calm his breathing while he imagined telling off Dennis, the townspeople supporting him all the way.

He had done it. He had done something that no one else in Two Lakes had ever done, not even Tom. The neighborhood kids would tell their parents about his triumph, and they would tell the other parents. By Monday morning, the farmers would be crowing about the newest superstar over their early morning coffee at the gas station. Kennedy estimated that his father would hear of his feat by the end of the week. He smiled as he realized that his dad might come back for him as early as next weekend.

"Kennedy," Harold whispered in his ear. "Kennedy, are you okay?"

Kennedy didn't open his eyes. "Sure, man. No problem." His voice was hoarse from the exertion.

"Are you gonna tell us about it—I mean what was out there and all?" Harold's babyish voice was soothing in its eagerness.

It was just the beginning. People would come from all over the county to see the boy who swam out to the cross. After his dad returned to Two Lakes, he would pull Kennedy to him, his arm tight around his son's shoulders, his admiration and pride spreading his smile even wider. He would return and they would be a family. A real family. A complete family.

"Just a short swim, that's all." He laughed to himself and listened to the water lapping up to the sand. He felt a connection to that water, fear and respect mingled into an understanding of the secret power it held. A power he beat.

He put his hands behind his head, snuggling deeper into the warm sand, trying to picture what his dad looked like. He must have dark hair, like his own, because his mother's hair was light. He must be tall and intelligent and always happy. He must miss Kennedy and regret leaving when Kennedy was still an infant. Kennedy knew he would have a good reason for leaving, even though his mother refused to talk about it.

"Kennedy, you...you...well, that was cool!"

Kennedy felt the summer sand shift as Tom sat next to him on the beach. Harold thumped on his other side, and the three of them sat enjoying the sun and the victory.

Kennedy laughed deep in his throat. "That was awfully cool, wasn't it?" He thought about his mom. She would be angry. No, she would pretend to be angry, just to make the neighbors think she was a good parent. No one lets their kids do such crazy stunts. But at home, hidden from the giddy public, she would hug him and rub his head and tell him how proud she was of him. "What do you think Dennis will say when he finds out?"

"Man, he won't say nothing." Tom laughed and Kennedy felt him roll over in the sand. "He won't believe it, of course."

"But we'll tell him, right Tom?" Harold interjected. "We'll tell him and everybody will know the truth."

Kennedy went back to thinking about his father, parading down Main Street with Kennedy on his shoulders. Maybe they would finally rename Main Street. Kennedy Street tasted sweet on his tongue, and he repeated it over and over in his mind, feeling the sounds on the tip of his tongue.

The sand lightened beside him, and a moment later Kennedy heard the water change, no longer calm, lying in wait for another soul to dare its secrets. He frowned. He heard the water fighting a new intruder.

"Oh, no. Not again," Harold said.

Kennedy sat up and blinked away the bright shards of sunlight stabbing his eyes. He slowly focused on a figure clumsily swimming out toward the cross. He looked around and realized it was Tom.

Kennedy thought he must be dreaming, must have fallen into a light sleep on the warm sand and was now imagining Tom trying to top his success. He wished it were a dream, but he knew it wasn't. He ignored his aching muscles and stood to watch Tom climb onto the cross, wave at the shore, then dive straight down into the water. He felt the pit of his stomach drop and begin a slow, acidic burn.

He waited for Tom to reappear. He counted five, ten, fifteen seconds, but Tom didn't reappear. He started counting again at one, thinking he must have miscounted. He reached seven before Tom's head popped up just a few feet from the cross. Kennedy let out his breath in a slow hiss as the burning in his stomach intensified.

Tom climbed up onto the cross and Kennedy realized he had been outdone. Tom hadn't even let him have his fanfare, hadn't given him a chance to be the hero, hadn't let the news of his triumph reach his father's ears. No one would hear of Kennedy's swim. No one would carry him through town. No one would be proud of his daring.

Kennedy watched Tom swim back to the shore. He wished the monsters would reach up and snag him from the surface, dragging him down to suffocate him under the weight of the water. But Tom emerged a moment later, smiling, his shoulders thrown back proudly as he walked right up to Kennedy. He reached out a hand to show Kennedy a smooth gray stone.

"What do you think of this one? I picked it up off the roof of the church. Neat, huh?" He showed it to Harold, who looked at it closely but didn't touch it. Kennedy stared at Tom. "It was lodged under one of the shingles. Man, it's a mess down there." Tom smiled and pushed past Kennedy, shaking water off his head.

Kennedy bit down on his lip, willing himself not to cry. He was still in Tom's shadow, where he had always been and where he would always be. It was a shadow that cloaked him in shame, hidden from his father's sight.

He turned and ran after Tom, pushing him down into the sand. "You jerk! You first-class A-one jerk!" Kennedy yelled. "Why did you do that? Why couldn't you let me be number one just for a little while?"

Tom stood up and spun around to face Kennedy. Harold took three steps back before tripping and falling to the ground.

Tom's eyebrows bent down to his nose and his mouth turned white around the edges. "What's your problem? You swam out there."

"Yeah, I swam out there first, but you—you went down below!" Kennedy hissed the last two words, afraid that whatever lived below the water would wake up at these words and come on to the beach to get them all. "I'll never get any respect now, not from Dennis, not from town, not from—" He swallowed the sentence before his anger betrayed his secret.

Tom moved to stand just inches from Kennedy. "Not from your daddy? You think your daddy would come back for you if you swam out there?" Tom barked a laugh. "Holy shit you're as stupid as Harold."

Kennedy refused to look away from Tom's cold stare. "You don't know anything," he said, barely a whisper. "You've got a dad."

Tom looked at Kennedy without moving. Kennedy wondered if the whole world had stopped moving, but he was afraid to break Tom's stare. He reminded himself to breathe.

"Yeah I do." Tom said it simply, only his lips moving. He blinked, a long slow blink. "You want that asshole? Take him." He shook his head. "Jesus, Kennedy. You can be so dense sometimes." He wiped his nose with the back of his hand. "Harold?"

A tiny "yeah?" came from Harold's space on the beach. Kennedy and Tom continued to look at each other, unmoving.

"Harold, you know what we just saw?" Tom didn't wait for an answer.

He took a step toward Kennedy, and Kennedy wanted to step back, but his feet got tangled together and he stayed where he was. Tom stretched out his hand, and Kennedy extended his own. Tom dropped the smooth stone onto Kennedy's palm.

"We just saw Kennedy do something really amazing, something no one else in this town has ever done." Tom stepped closer to Kennedy and tilted his eyes up slightly. "Wow," he whispered.

He threw back his head and cackled, causing both Kennedy and Harold to jump. He slapped Kennedy on the shoulder and turned to Harold. "Let's go spread the news." He signaled to the older boy to follow him to their bikes. Harold shrugged at Kennedy, then followed Tom.

Kennedy stayed on the beach, the cold stone burning in his hand. He didn't look at it as his fingers closed over it, squeezing it so tightly that he thought he might crush it. He knew. Somehow he knew. Maybe it was the way his mother never talked about his father or the way no one in the town ever talked about fathers around him, but he knew he would never see his father.

He opened his palm and looked at the stone. It wasn't as flawless as it had felt in his palm. It had small black grooves on one side and a deep gash in the middle. The coloring was actually waves of white and gray swirling and mingling. He couldn't see where the two colors were distinctly different, couldn't see a definite boundary between the two, but he could see the different colors.

He wondered if Tom's dad was proud of his son. He closed his palm again, then threw the stone back into the lake. He would let his monsters sleep just a bit longer.

Part II:

Honeysuckle Memories

LOST AND FOUND

J ane Dixon, please report to the information desk to pick up your lost item. Jane Dixon, please report to the information desk to pick up your lost item."

I sit on the plain gray carpet in an obscure corner near gate D52 of the St. Louis airport and wonder what Jane has left behind during her travels. My afternoon flight to Omaha has already been delayed to early evening. The stewardesses haven't arrived from a connecting flight. Two hundred waiting passengers mingle in a confining area with forty occupied chairs and limited floor space, although the prime real estate is near the solitary silver ashtray that marks the smoking area.

The waiting passengers seem anxious to get on the plane and start their Thanksgiving holiday of stuffing their faces and recovering the next day with leftovers and a football game between the eleventh-ranked Cornhuskers and the third-ranked Sooners. In their minds, annihilation is the only possible outcome and I shake my head that the buzz from beating Kansas continues even two weeks later. Wannabe cadets dressed in the clean blue uniform of their private military school celebrate their temporary freedom, chattering about whether Billy Todd will break another field goal record for Nebraska. One cadet, too young to know about pimples, shoves a greasy hot dog from the overpriced snack shop into his mouth before chasing his cohorts. The screaming orange lights herald speeding carts painfully pushing their way through crowds of people reluctant to give up their precious share of space. A young girl talks on the pay phone at the end of the row of chairs nearest me, annoying the people around her with her breathless account of her new college life and how she can see the football practices from her dorm window so she knows that the team is no match for the Cornhuskers.

The polite voice interrupts the elevator music and calmly repeats the request to Jane Dixon to claim her lost item.

Waves of people are blocking the airport corridor, trying to board at the next gate. The sign says Ft. Lauderdale and I am curious who is traveling south for the holiday. There are no fat people in line. Fat people must not go to Ft. Lauderdale. I wish I were going to invigorating Florida, where a cold day doesn't require a heavy winter coat and where sunshine isn't a pleasant surprise on a winter day. My bleak trip to snowy Nebraska will be dominated by strangers with affected looks of pity at the memorial service for my mother and by my grandmother's drunken eyes full of tears and hidden weaknesses. My grandmother is such a thoughtful, caring woman. If we catch her after happy hour, which starts around ten in the morning at her house. Of course, now that her only remaining child has died, I am sure the drinking will start much earlier. And along with her medicinal benefits of the CC and 7's will come the blurred speeches about losing all her children to such a dreadful disease as cancer, but they're in a better place now, no more unnecessary suffering, and why does everyone have to leave so quickly when it's obvious that the family is in turmoil and can't everyone stay just a few weeks to help the grandchildren—think of the children!—get through this terrible loss? And when she pauses to take another gulp I will assure her that we will be fine, that we will throw ourselves into our work, oblivious to the world around us, or finish up our schooling, especially since we are so close to graduating, or maybe even finally commit to that special relationship and start practicing to produce our own little bundles of joy that will be ripped from our arms before we are ready to let go. And if I am feeling particularly frustrated and my patience is abandoning me, I will offer to freshen up her drink and maybe take a few hits myself. And I think maybe I should go to the snack bar around the corner for a quick shot of vodka before my plane takes off to help take the chill off the trip.

Phone girl has finished her account of college life and is slurping down a 7Up from the snack bar. I hope she gets a brain freeze. Another cadet walks by with a bag of stale-smelling popcorn and tries to find a place to sit down. He wanders into the smoking section, past a group of green-faced men huddled around a solitary silver ashtray, rehashing the game with Kansas and explaining how the offensive team will steamroll Oklahoma, just like they did Kansas. The men smile and laugh grotesquely, expelling a cloud of smoke above their heads. I want to jump up and scream at them. I want to run over and grab their shirts and shake them back and forth until their eyes roll back and their necks snap to the weight of their fat heads. I want to punch them and kick them and ask them how they can be so incredibly stupid to voluntarily forfeit their lives to this disgusting toxin. I want to know why their polluted asses are still here, embracing life, while my mother was stolen from me. My mother, who had an innocent childhood fear of alligators hiding under her bed at night, who made me wear that God-awful pink polyester dress for picture day in the first grade just so she could pull it out years later for my boyfriends to smirk over, who used a cartoon book with funny naked people to explain the joy of sex, and who introduced me to the wonderful experience of a gynecological exam. My mother, who bought me the new Shawn Cassidy album when I struck out and lost the championship softball game for my team, who let me learn to drive on her brand new AMC Pacer, who encouraged me to take debate in high school so I could learn how to BS my way through life, and who suffered through three years of cancer without ever crying. She was taken from me before she could teach me everything about my unborn children, but these sick bastards with their halos of smoke and indifference to others stand in the crowd of holiday travelers and publicly flaunt their power over nicotine. They have a haughty look that they are beating the drug, it won't hurt them, and they puff and blow smoke into the air, into the face of a baby in overalls sitting nearby.

The baby screams, his face turning red. *Good for him, scream louder. Scream until their eardrums burst and they agonize in pain.* The baby's mother picks him up, trying to comfort him. He screams louder, his mouth gaping, eyes squished shut, cheeks flaming. The smokers look uncomfortable and satisfaction whispers in my ear.

But please, God, don't that kid be on my flight.

The polite voice cuts into the soothing saxophone music to remind us that Jane Dixon still hasn't picked up her lost item. I wish that anonymous voice would page me to retrieve what I have lost. My mother's voice echoes her familiar advice in my head: Life isn't fair but we deal with what we have—that's what makes us human. And I know I must forget my anger and move on because that is what she would have wanted me to do. That is what would make her proud. I pull out my ticket and look at my seat number. 9F. A window seat. I inhale the smell of greasy hot dogs, stale smoke, and fusty gray carpet and stand up. I shoulder my bag and head for the gate. I get in line behind three middle-aged businessmen and in front of the woman with the red-faced baby and I pretend to be human.

TILLY'S TEACUP

Tilly didn't sit down. She stood at the counter, wiping a damp sponge back and forth along the clean sink edge, rubbing her tongue along the groove where her front teeth had been before they rotted out. It was a nasty habit that made her look like a fish puckering her upper lip, but the monotony of the action calmed her. She didn't have anyone to impress in this dying farm town. She took a gulp of freshly brewed coffee, burning the skin on the roof of her mouth. She dropped the coffee mug back to the counter and danced around the kitchen in pain, tripping on the unused cat dish and cursing her stupidity.

She sat down at her Formica table, curling her toes and rubbing her knuckles into her knees to force the pain out of her mouth. She wasn't supposed to be drinking or eating anything anyway, but her coffee was such an ingrained habit. Like breathing. She glanced at the small brown box on her table, then jumped back up to stand at the counter.

The grandfather clock in the living room struck a chord. The kitchen clock said 6:45.

She should be leaving now. She resumed her sink cleaning and picked at dead skin with her tongue. She tried to convince herself the mist of sweat on her upper lip was from the coffee. Maybe it was hot flashes. She snorted. She had finished all that years ago. Tilly looked around her kitchen. She cleaned it every day, sometimes twice a day, but everything looked so worn. And gray. She had been so proud when her husband had redone the whole kitchen for her, bringing in a crackle-white refrigerator and a self-cleaning stove. But her husband had been dead for thirty-two years now. They never had kids. Her kitchen had become a desolate tomb where she spent most of her time.

Tilly sighed and glanced at the wall clock. 6:49. She really needed to leave now.

She picked up the cat dish and laughed. The Cat had run away long ago. Tilly never gave the Siamese mix a name, just The Cat. He would watch Tilly clean the house and listen to stories about her dead husband and decomposing house. She slumped over to the table and sat down. She missed The Cat. She dropped the dust-filled dish on the table, next to the plain brown box waiting to be opened.

She already knew what was in the box. She spent her weekly allowance on it. She had gone to cash her social security check to get money for groceries and the electric bill and this morning's doctor bill. But she had been drawn into the antique store instead. She carefully set the box in front of her.

Breathe. In two three, out two three.

She opened what the antique dealer had so lovingly wrapped. Folds of crisp white tissue paper blossomed into a small blue teacup. She pulled it out of the box and set it on its saucer in front of her. The box and wrappings dropped to the linoleum next to her chair.

6:53. If she left now, she would only be a few minutes late. She frowned. She hated the clinic's waiting rooms.

A deep expulsion of breath pushed her deeper into her chair and she tried to remember why she had spent $45 on the dainty cup. $45.27 to be exact. When she asked to see the cup, she'd been flooded with memories of drinking honeysuckle tea with her mother. Tilly had barely been able to see over the table, but she loved to sit and watch her mother bake the bread that she sold to their neighbors, always sitting down for a cup of tea before starting the next order.

The clerk spoke in a nasally voice, telling her they discontinued the deep blue of the cup after only one year. That didn't make it worth the money she had wasted. The ticking of the clock invaded her thoughts. She mumbled "shut up" at the clock, but looked at it anyway.

6:55. They had stressed to her not to be late.

She leaned her elbows on the table and dropped her head into her hands, rubbing her temples with her thumbs, tracing the pea-sized mole on her left temple. She felt the coarse gray hairs and laughed at the absurdity that a mole would have more hair than she had on her head. Well, maybe that was an exaggeration, but not by much. Age had created ruffles of sagging skin in places she never knew could sag. And if it wasn't sagging, it was splattered with rusty age spots. Of course, then there were those spots that had both sagged and rusted.

Tilly looked at the teacup through her fingers. She was not supposed to be late for the appointment. They had stuck a six-inch needle into the lump in her breast, smiled as they told her it was cancerous, and cheerfully informed her of an available time to have it removed, as if she were visiting a fancy spa like the one Samantha treated her friends to on "Sex and the City." Tilly blushed. Her sister-in-law gave her the entire series for Christmas several years ago. Tilly had forced herself to watch all the episodes so she could have something to talk about with her sister-in-law, but she hadn't seen her husband's family since receiving the DVD set.

7:01. Maybe she should call and tell them she was running late.

She wanted to talk to someone about the tumor, the huge tumor, the mammoth tumor, the tumor that had hooked its claws into her breast. Her husband had always been too busy reading newspapers in his overstuffed chair to be much of a listener, but even his disinterested mumbles would be reassuring now. Even The Cat's soft blue eyes following her around the house would chase away some of the solitude. She could call one of the other volunteers at the Food Bank or someone from the Senior Citizen Center.

No, she wouldn't call anyone. She only exchanged tedious greetings and pleasantries with those people anyway. She didn't want to see in their faces that she, sagging and rusting Tilly, was dying. So far only she knew what was happening, only she felt the pulsing tumor every second of her decaying life.

But maybe she was imagining it all.

She looked at the teacup and pictured the tumor. She knew it was big. She had almost become accustomed to it swelling and pressing against her inner arm in the two years since she had first noticed it. It was probably as big as this special teacup. She envisioned the deep blue teacup filled with the tumor, filled to the brim, so that watery pus-yellow sludge oozed over the edge and down into the saucer. She didn't know if it would actually be yellow, but it was something that happened with age. Her tumor would be a nice faded-newspaper yellow. Probably with some hints of rust. She fingered the delicate handle of the cup, worried that her clumsy fingers might break it, snapping it like a brittle wafer cookie.

7:11. Tilly couldn't remember how much they charged for the appointment.

She didn't have any money left. Maybe they would accept the teacup instead of money. She cradled the teacup back into its box and packed it back into the crisp white tissue.

She went to the counter, breathing in the smell of cooling coffee. She picked up her ivory rotary dial phone and grabbed the phone book resting underneath.

She glanced in the mirror hanging on the wall, then quickly looked away. She didn't want to see her missing front teeth and hairy mole and thinning hair and yellow death. She opened the phone book and ripped out the page listing the animal shelter and nearby vets, folded it neatly, and pressed it into the pocket of her jacket. She would need reading material for the doctor's waiting room.

THE TEN-YEAR GOD

She shoved her red lace panties into her Jesus is the Reason tote, then threw the jar of KamaSutra Honey Dust Powder and its accompanying feather applicator on the bed.

"Keep it. Think of me," she sneered, not looking at him. She strode out of the apartment, carrying the last of her belongings. She refused to look back.

She dropped the tote into the passenger seat, pulled out into the early morning traffic, and jammed her foot onto the gas pedal, ready to expunge the last decade from her memory. Unfortunately the commuters were not sympathetic to her plight and she found herself staring down a long line of cars waiting for a green light.

She tried to distract herself by studying the people in the neighboring cars, the clouds forming in the sky, the grass growing in the median—anything to keep her from looking back to see if he had followed her out. She envisioned him standing on the building steps, wondering if he had made a mistake. She wouldn't give him the satisfaction.

She spied a steeple peeking up between a congregation of buildings. She snorted, thanking God they had not gone that route. Her friends had one by one fallen victim to the mass-marketed cure to the Being Single disease, giving up their savings accounts, their studies, their fast track to a management position to men who didn't seem nearly as invested in the relationship, all in an effort to hide their deep-seated insecurities about never being loved.

She shook her head. She had sworn that would never become one of *those* kinds of women. She would not forsake her career, her dreams, her identity for any man, no matter how good he could fuck. It was her father's only legacy to her, handed down to her when he walked out of the hospital and into anonymity as her mother screamed in labor. No, she would never equate being alone with being lonely.

Growing up in loving, two-parent families had made her friends weak. Inevitably they had all called her in tears, outraged and hurt that their men had not provided the expected fairy tale ending that Disney promised. She had silently laughed at them, knowing that their fury was the acceptable facade for their failure, hiding their mortification at the all-too-visible recurrence of BS disease.

Now she laughed out loud at them, glancing in her rear view mirror. "Shit!"

He wasn't there. He wasn't on the steps, hoping she'd come back and convince him that he was wrong.

The dark blue Buick in front of her inched forward as the light turned green, and she inched right along with it.

"C'mon, c'mon," she said, willing the cars through the intersection. She moved forward several feet before the light turned red and the line of cars rolled to a stop. She groaned loudly, gripped the wheel until her knuckles were white, then dropped her head against her knuckles.

"Fuck."

The anger drained from her. She had turned into one of them. She had stayed in the relationship long after it had soured. She had known from day one that they would never be a real couple, a committed couple, a Cosby Show couple. But she had been pursuing her master's degree at the time and needed to blow off some steam. And the sex had been too good to pass up. She'd told herself not to romanticize it, even while boarding a plane to follow him home to Brazil, abandoning her studies with just six credit hours to go. But how could she not? She was following her lover to another country, proving her commitment to him.

For ten years she had seen only what she wanted to see in the relationship—a hidden caress, a meaningful glance in a crowded room, whispered passions in the bedroom—while ignoring the fact that outside the bedroom, they had no relationship. They didn't talk about world events or go to movies with friends or plan a future. They fucked. And it was good. But she could get the same pleasure from a vibrator.

She inhaled deeply as she leaned back, wondering if the traffic was her penance for a decade of living in sin. No, her God wouldn't deny her the pleasures of the flesh, although He would chastise her for putting a skillful tongue and well-maneuvered cock before Him. He might also point out the irony. She exhaled, letting her anger go. She had made her choices. She didn't regret them. She certainly wasn't a failure because she now had to make new choices, nor could she be humiliated because she was in the single lane again.

She grabbed the red panties from her bag as the light turned green. The line of cars surged. She rolled down her window while keeping close to the Buick in front of her.

She sailed through the intersection, dropping the panties out the window and thanking God for her incurable BS disease.

TWENTY MINUTES

I have a secret. I want my grandmother to die. I glance at my watch as I push the door to her room barely open. *Twenty minutes. Just twenty minutes. Unless she's asleep, and then I'll wait until next week.* Although in reality I hope that a visit next week won't be necessary.

I peek through the crack in the door, into the gray room. Maybe she's asleep. A twinge of hope shoots up my spine. My eyes aren't adjusting quickly enough. I listen for a moment, for her movements or her breathing. I hear nothing. I hold my breath. Maybe she's dead.

"Who's there?"

I see her form now, a tiny figure drowning in the hospital bed. *Damn.* I push the door, telling myself to smile, act happy. I say hello.

"Who are you?"

I move closer to the hospital bed, praying that somewhere in her lost mind my grandmother doesn't realize my smile is fake. "It's me, Nana. Alex."

I want my voice to be soothing and kind, but it seems empty to me. She is propped up against a jumbo off-white pillow, looking at an empty space six inches in front of her, her head hanging slightly to the left in a permanent droop.

"Nana, how are you today?" *Tell me something is wrong, your back hurts or you're having trouble breathing. Tell me your body is finally catching up with your soul as it rushes toward another life.*

"I don't know you." She flinches, and her right hand suddenly starts smoothing invisible wrinkles from her faded flowered dress. Her left hand remains stationary, loosely curled into a ball on her lap. Both wrists are bound with black restraints. She is mumbling. "I don't know you. Go away."

"Nana, I'm your granddaughter." I enunciate each word, as if talking to someone who doesn't speak my language.

I rest my hands on the guard rail of the hospital bed. Her hand continues to smooth. Twenty minutes might have been an overly ambitious goal. If machines were keeping her alive, I could trip on a cord, pulling it out of the socket. But her body is a traitor, and I resist the rage stinging in my throat at the unfairness.

I take a deep breath, place my hand on her arm, and try again. "I'm Richard's daughter."

Her hand stops suddenly, apparently satisfied that the wrinkle has vanished. I wait, wanting her to react yet afraid she might. She doesn't move, and it seems even her breathing has stopped. I look at her chest and cross my fingers in my mind. I count to four before I see her chest slowly rise.

I jerk my hand away, afraid I might punch her. Or worse.

"Daughters," she whispers. Her voice crackles. "I have daughters."

Twenty-pound weights drop on my shoulders, and I feel exhausted. I don't want to deal with her today, her false memories. I am sick of explaining life to her. She doesn't remember her family, her childhood home, her first kiss, what she had for lunch thirty minutes ago. I thank God she doesn't remember taking care of her own sister as she battled Alzheimer's for seventeen years. I just as quickly beg Him not to let Nana cling to life that long.

"No, Nana. You don't have any daughters."

I reach out across her lap and put my hand on top of hers. It's cold, and I wonder why there are no blankets in the private room. She jerks her hand out from under mine and yanks against the restraints.

"Daughters!" she screams, her right hand clawing at the air, trying to grab and scratch and rip. Her head doesn't move, but her chest heaves and her legs kick against unseen restraints. "I have daughters!"

I jump back, taken off guard, She kicks and pulls and grunts for several moments, and I relax as her movements belie her fatigue. She is breathing hard, wheezing, and I think the tantrum is finished. But she starts again.

"You bitch," she hisses, but she is still focused on that space in front of her.

I don't react. The doctors have told me time and again that there is nothing I can do except wait for her anger to pass.

"You filthy bitch!" Spittle runs down her flushed face and she strains harder. "Who are you? What did you do to them?"

I stand back and try to ignore her. I look around the room, at the bare beige walls, the lonely black chair in the corner, the dust-covered TV. It is identical to my mother's hospital room, except for the chair, which was brown and was constantly in use.

My grandmother is still straining against the straps, grunting, veins popping out all along her arms. It's a disgusting sight. I turn to look at the door, but no nurse comes in to check on us.

"You killed them—you killed my babies!" My grandmother is screaming again, her voice splintering into hoarse air and spit. "I hate you! Get out! Get out!" Red welts swell against the restraints, matching the surge of my anger.

I am furious—furious at a god who obviously screwed up the matching of bodies and souls. My grandmother's soul left years ago, but her body is tenacious. My mother's body invited cancer in, welcomed it, made it a permanent resident, and betrayed her soul, whose only wish was to see her own grandchildren born.

"You stupid old hag." I am surprised by the growl coming from my throat, but I make no effort to stop it. "Yes, your daughters are dead. Dead and buried in some nameless cemetery." I move closer to her bed, leaning down to hiss at her. "Why don't you go join them?" My face is burning and I grab the bed's railing, wringing the cold metal as if it were her neck. Finally, the rage explodes from my chest. "Just hurry up and die!"

I glare at her, daring her to move, ready to pounce, wishing she would give me any reason to throttle her. But we are both motionless, save for our harmonious panting, each waiting for the other to act.

"Who are you?" she asks, her voice quiet and timid.

I can hear her fear. I drop my face into my hands and shriek in exasperation. I rub my eyes, trying to rub out all the bitterness and anger. Finally, I look at her and sigh.

"Nana, it's me, Alex."

She doesn't react.

"I'm your granddaughter."

Her hand starts smoothing out the wrinkle again. "Granddaughter?" Her voice is serene. She wipes at her eye, streaking moisture across her cheek.

I look at my watch. Twenty minutes is up.

THE CONTAMINATION OF
JUNE CLEAVER

Margaret looked away from the table as Grace produced two mugs, followed by fresh-baked chocolate chip cookies. The smell induced another wave of nausea, and Margaret grabbed her coffee and forced down a gulp of the burning liquid. She had kept a tight control on her nerves all night, but she was tired and her body was betraying her. She had to tell Grace. Grace would fix it, make it right. She always did.

"Thank God she's finally getting married," Grace said, sitting down at the table. "Sometimes I think Angela scares men off before she even meets them. She's so insecure." She shook her head, then took a sip of coffee. "Drink some coffee. You look awful. You're getting too old to party all night."

"Yeah." Margaret sat up straighter, clearing her throat.

Spill it. Now. Tell her everything. Start with the party and the ride home and the rest will follow. Just start. Say it. Say something.

Margaret took another drink of coffee. "Yeah."

"I'm so glad I found Lucas for her." Grace set her coffee cup down and Margaret felt the headache from last night coming back. "So how do you like working with your future brother-in-law?"

Margaret shrugged, trying to paste a fake smile on her lips.

Tell her about it. Tell her about the five o'clock Fridays, blowing off steam, having to listen to his sick sex jokes where the women are always objects to be used by the male victor.

"Someone to share the daily grind," Margaret said, adding a hollow laugh.

Tell her about the ride home, Lucas rattling on and on about how to ask Angela, what to say, grabbing Margaret's hand, squeezing it—he was so nervous—and not letting go.

She took another sip of coffee and hoped Grace noticed her hands shaking.

"I'm just thrilled this one has a job." Grace laughed as she tore a piece from a still warm cookie and popped it in her mouth. She stood up to grab a bleached-white dishtowel from the edge of the sink.

"Yeah, so Angela can work full time on controlling her emotions," Margaret said, mumbling as Grace wiped an errant crumb from the table and deposited it in the trash.

Grace sat back down and patted Margaret on the arm. "Just get it all out of your system before she shows up."

Margaret bit down despite the soreness in her jaw. "She's coming today?" Hyperventilating. Tears. Nausea. Migraine. The sickness was waking, and it was pissed about being disturbed yet again. "When?"

Grace cocked her head to the side, and Margaret knew she'd finally gotten her attention.

"Oh, you, just relax." She smiled, holding her coffee cup with both hands as if she were about to drink the elixir. "She'll be too excited to start anything today." Grace locked her eyes on Margaret, giving her the *that goes for you too* stare that Margaret endured at least once during every visit.

Margaret bit her tongue and closed her eyes, her stomach clenched, and she screamed at her body to keep in control. Grace would fix it. Grace fixed everything. She'd clean it all up, a true matriarch, having stepped into their mother's shoes so fluidly, even without anyone asking her to take over. And she did it all with a picture-perfect smile and never a hair out of place.

Margaret held a hand over her mouth. She was going to puke all over the pristine table with its homemade cookies that would make Martha Stewart jealous. She focused her thoughts on Grace, willing her to ask the question so Margaret could tell her about the scratches, the bruises, the helplessness.

But Grace just smiled in her perfect June Cleaver way, her face a beautiful blank canvas.

Margaret swallowed and forced the muscles in her throat to relax. She tried to remain calm, putting her body into a meditative stillness.

"He kissed me." She didn't feel her lips move, but Grace's smile stayed perfect just a second too long. "And more." She looked down into her coffee and begged for someone—a higher power, the old puppeteer upstairs—to grant her this one dignity, save her a tidbit of control.

Grace inhaled deeply, paused, then wiped at the spotless table with her carefully ironed dishtowel. "A quick kiss between friends, future in-laws." Her whitened fingers pushed the towel harder, scouring the already gleaming table, as if pushing the idea away from her, away from the table, and out the window.

"No." Margaret shook her head. She suddenly wanted another shower, wanted her older sister to bleach the stains from her mind until she was crisp and fresh and new again. Her tears fell, and she smiled. She let them cover her face, washing off his salty beer-breath slobber until it spread all over Grace's perfect white table. She breathed in sharply and blew out the stale smell of his cheap cologne. "Oh,

Grace, he did so much more." She buried her face in her arms on the cool table.

Just fix it, Grace, please. Tell Angela. Call off the wedding. Angela won't believe it, not from me, never from me. She'll think I'm trying to steal another one, trying to ruin her life again. But you can convince her.

Margaret sat up and felt light-headed. She looked at Grace, whose flawless smile seemed to wilt just a hair before righting itself.

"He gave me a ride home, from the office, from happy hour. He was nervous. About asking her. He grabbed my hand." She wiped at her nose, but it wouldn't stop running. "He wouldn't let go."

Grace stood, handed Margaret a lace-edged handkerchief produced from a hidden pocket, and turned to the counter. A moment later, she was filling Margaret's nearly full coffee cup. "Oh, sweetie, are you jealous?" The words were measured and direct, but Grace's eyes were darting around the kitchen, as if virtually scouring the dust particles from the cabinets and walls. "Don't worry, you're young. You'll find your Prince Charming." She returned the coffee pot to its place and smoothed non-existent wrinkles from her apron. "Let's not go through this again. Let Angela have her moment." She smiled a perfect pearly row of teeth.

But Margaret heard Lucas's laugh telling her how nervous he was while licking his lips. Red blotches burned up Margaret's arms, and she thanked the puppeteer for at last covering the bruises and scratches from Lucas's stubby fingers and greasy nails. She glared at her sister, repulsed by her sterile home.

"He tried so much," Margaret hissed, "but I pushed him away. He grabbed me, said I wanted it too, and the fucking car doors were locked and I couldn't pull away." Her sister flinched at the language. Margaret smiled. "He tried. Do you understand? He tried, but I fought him. I fought the bastard—me, I fought him! Do you understand?" She wanted Grace to understand, wanted her to tell Angela so their sister could escape before it was too late.

Grace exhaled a deep breath. She sat down and crossed her arms on the table. She looked at Margaret for a long moment. "He's a man. Men do these things. But you're okay." Grace leaned over the table. "Angela will take care of him. Don't ruin this for her." She picked up the plate of cookies and held it in front of Margaret. "Have a cookie. You'll feel better."

And Margaret was dismissed.

She stared at her sister's perfectly coiffed hair and unfaltering smile and saw her June Cleaver reality, where everything was black and white with none of Margaret's grays or Angela's reds and yellows.

Margaret closed her eyes, but his laughter echoed in her head. She had tried to warn them. Grace didn't want to know. Grace was supposed to fix it. She fixed everything. But she couldn't fix this. Or wouldn't.

Margaret swallowed more coffee, hoping it would burn away the memories of him ripping at her clothes. Even as she hoped it, she knew it was futile.

She opened her eyes. She would have to be the matriarch now.

PART III:

HONEYSUCKLE DREAMS

AFTERMATH

Six days after the Twin Towers fell, American airports remained abandoned, relics of an era that evaporated in the space of 102 minutes. I felt like an intruder. The clipping of my high heels echoed throughout the Dallas/Fort Worth International Airport. Airport personnel no longer had the bored look I had become accustomed to. Instead, their dark icy stares pierced my invisible armor. I fought the urge to run from their hawkish eyes.

I was the first to arrive at my gate. A few moments later, a burly redneck with thinning hair sat down in the waiting area. He studied me, his bright blue eyes carrying out their own strip search. I crossed my arms over my chest and turned away from him. It was not my decision to travel. I would have preferred to remain ensconced in my isolation, waiting to see what happened next, secure within the coastal grey walls of my one-bedroom house on the edge of a tiny town that doesn't exist on any map.

Two airport security personnel approached the waiting area, their hands positioned on large automatic guns in a way that said "I don't have to shoot you, but I could." They stopped at the redneck first, asking to see his boarding pass and ID. When they turned to me, I had my documents ready.

"You just bought this ticket yesterday."

The backup officer's hands clenched his gun more tightly.

I nodded.

The redneck sneered at me and said "Jesus."

The officer frowned. "Explain."

"My sister," I said, adopting the same laconic manner. "Car accident. Bad outlook."

It wasn't exactly the truth, but that didn't matter. The officer asked for details—names, location, hospital—then turned so that his gun was pointed at my throat. After several back-and-forth calls with security headquarters, his partner confirmed the information. The officer handed my documents back, and they moved on to the next waiting area.

"Sorry about your sister," the redneck said.

I nodded in fake appreciation. She wasn't my sister. We had been best friends since second grade. It was a friendship borne from a small-town context rather than undying commitment to one another. We had just always hung out together.

Until she got married.

The flight attendants arrived. A handful of passengers shuffled in behind them. Redneck and I wouldn't be alone on the flight. The crew asked us to sit in the first ten rows of seats during the flight. I realized they wanted to keep an eye on us. The airlines were trying to get back to business as usual, but business was damn jumpy for those in the air, surrounded by a bunch of strangers, with no viable exit strategy.

Exit strategies were always a bitch.

I slept through the ninety-minute flight and was still groggy when we deplaned. The crew looked relieved. I did not share in their sentiment. Within twenty minutes of landing, I was driving my rental car west on Highway 36. An hour later, the sun had set and I stood outside her hospital room, the smell of disinfectant tickling my nose.

I was afraid to go in. Everything was happening way too fast. What was I doing here?

There really had been a car accident, and my best friend really was in critical condition. My mother called to tell me about it as soon as she heard, and I booked a ticket out on the next available flight. I did it without thinking, never considering that my friend probably didn't want to see me.

I heard a deep voice talking to someone at the nurses' station just down the hall and I realized that I hadn't come for her, my best friend. I'd come for Jimmy, her husband.

If I hadn't heard him talking, I don't think I would have recognized his gritty unshaven face and sunken eyes. His hair had more salt than pepper, and I wanted to tease him about getting old as I ran my fingers through his tousled hair and pulled him in for a deep exploratory kiss.

He could never say no to my kisses.

Instead I watched him walk down the hall, a cup of coffee in one hand, his other shoved into the pocket of deeply stained jeans. He glanced at me, and I blinked back tears, stung by his lack of recognition.

"Jimmy," I said, my voice scratched and husky from traveling.

Recognition clicked and without breaking stride he pulled me into a tight one-armed hug that felt so comfortable, so intimate. I relaxed into him, and he held on to me even tighter. "Thank you for coming," he whispered into my ear. I tried to ignore the thrill it sent down my spine.

He pulled back, and my body cried out in frustration.

"How's she doing?" My breathing was stilted. I hoped he didn't notice.

He cocked his head toward the door. "Come, say hello."

As he held the door open, I opened my mouth to say something, then closed it, afraid I would puke all over the pristine hospital floor. I swallowed hard, pushing my nausea down into the pit of my stomach, and tried again. "Is she awake?" My voice squeaked. Even I didn't hear what came out.

I took a step forward, already cringing at what I might find. An image came to mind of the people jumping from the Twin Towers, preferring a 100-story jump to the fiery planes in their offices. My mind was screaming at me to run, bolt, about face and just get out, anything but face what was on the other side of that door.

Jimmy pulled me in.

That was how it had all started in the first place, with him pulling me in. But I let myself be pulled in, just like always.

The body in the bed didn't look like anyone I knew. The face and arms—at least the parts that weren't wrapped in bright white gauze—were deep red with mottled purples and yellows. Wires connected her wrists and hands to machines that beeped in greeting.

Jimmy stood beside me. "We're unplugging everything in the morning. I just wanted another night."

"Where is everyone? Her parents?"

He shook his head. "This is my night, my chance to say goodbye."

I turned to look at him. I needed to go, leave him in peace, suddenly hating myself for enjoying his hug while interrupting his mourning.

"No, stay." He pulled me by the elbow toward a loveseat across from the foot of the bed. "Fill me in."

"On what?" I sat on the edge of the cushion and tried to ignore the body in the room, but I was constantly checking the bed, waiting for her to sit up and talk.

"Life," he said. He smiled. "Love." He held my hand in both of his, resting it lightly on his knee as his thumb rubbed up and down my finger. "Have you found it?"

I couldn't breathe past the lump in my throat. Was this a trick question? I shook my head and shrugged at the same time, creating a jerking kind of movement that didn't feel intelligible.

"She's missed you." He smiled and pushed a lock of hair from my face. "Me too."

I nodded, glancing back at the bed. "What happened?" I whispered.

He breathed in deeply, slowly. "She lost another one. Tomorrow would have been the second trimester."

I started to say I was sorry, but he shook me off.

"She wanted them, not me," he said. "I just wanted her to be happy."

I pulled my hand from his, now uncomfortable with the intimate action. I pretended to rummage around in my bag, looking for something. What I really wanted was time—time to digest everything. But I knew I had none.

"There's really nothing they can do?" I asked, not looking up from my bag.

He shook his head. "Her spine or brain is messed up. I can't remember which. They explained everything a couple of times."

I glanced up to see him looking at the bed. He chewed on his bottom lip—something I had once found endearing. Now it seemed too innocent, too child-like.

"Are you doing okay?" I asked.

He nodded. "We had a good run." He looked back at the bed, still nodding. "Yep, a good run."

I frowned. They'd only been married a few years—six? No, more like eight. I couldn't remember exactly and didn't want to go through the math. I didn't go to the wedding. I thought it was a joke. They got married a few weeks after their first date, right before Christmas. I started sleeping with Jimmy the following summer.

"She was upset, crying about losing it." He leaned back, put his hand on my back, rubbing up and down. "I told her I would come get her, but she didn't want to wait." His hand faltered on my back.

I groaned and dropped my head into my hands. I felt the cushion sink as he sat forward, draping his arm across my back and resting his chin on my shoulder.

"Hush now." His warm breath tickled my ear.

I remembered when he used to kiss my ears, his tongue and teeth teasing me until I would laugh and beg for more. He caught on that a few well-placed kisses would make me putty in his hands and used his knowledge at the most inopportune times—while swimming at the river, while driving down the highway, at the Superbowl party they hosted. I stifled a shudder remembering the Superbowl party. Chargers versus the 49ers. He pushed the limits, catching up to me in the hall, shoving me into their bathroom, and stealing a few minutes with me while his wife prepped more nachos and beer for the guests. San Diego scored their fourth touchdown while I bit his shoulder in silent climax.

It had been gloriously naughty.

And when I left to help with the food and drink, she looked at me and knew. She stared at me, the look in her eyes as cold as the airport security guys' guns pointed right at me. She didn't say anything. She didn't need to. I carried out two plates of nachos, set them on the table, then walked out the front door.

It was the last time I had seen either of them.

"Cops said she probably didn't even see the train," Jimmy said.

I was both grateful and angry that he interrupted my memories. But that was Jimmy. He was always playing both sides. He never tried to contact me after I left, yet here we were, six years later, as if we were still in the throes of our illicit affair.

"The train?" I turned to look at him. He nodded, and my knees turned to wet noodles. I looked at the bed, shaking my head.

She had joked about it when we were in high school, saying she didn't want to grow old, that she would park her car in front of a train on her fortieth birthday and take care of everything. Quick and neat. She said it out loud, explained her logic in great detail, and laughed as she did, but she avoided train crossings after that, driving miles out of her way so she wouldn't tempt fate.

"What did she say on the phone?"

He shrugged, rubbing my back once more. "She was crying. It was messy."

I jerked away from his hand.

He rolled his eyes and dropped his hands in his lap. He sighed. "She apologized, said she messed up again. Something about fixing it for me."

"Fixing it." I looked back at the bed. "For you."

"I told you. She was upset."

I nodded, glancing around. I stood up, grateful that my noodly legs didn't give way.

"You okay?"

I nodded. "Gonna go check into the hotel, grab a shower." I wanted to wash the entire day away.

He stood and walked me the few steps to the door, holding on to my elbow the entire time. At the doorway he turned me around and kissed me, a soft peck shared by friends that turned into a penetrating kiss in which he gave me everything he had, exposing his pain and fear while begging me to save him. And oh God how I wanted to save him—take him out to the rental car and frisk him away to cozy hideaway where no one would ever find us.

"Come by the house tomorrow," he said when he finally pulled away. His voice was like melted butter. I smiled and nodded.

But as I walked down the hospital corridor, I knew I would never see him again. Like I said, exit strategies are a bitch, but I took my cue from my best friend Laura and left without telling anyone goodbye.

Laura. Yes, I could say her name, dammit. But I knew that wasn't true either. I was like the caustic dust in the post-9/11 world, causing cancer for anyone who tried to help. Laura was no exception. I had hurt her, deeply, but so had her husband and she had stayed with him even after it all.

Husbands were supposed to cheat. I know that is how she would have rationalized it. Her own father had cheated on her mother. Laura walked in on him and the high school biology teacher, naked and moaning on the living room floor. She laughed as she told me that she stood there, waiting for them to finish, then thanked the teacher for giving her an A in class. I didn't completely believe her, but she never even opened her biology book and brought home an A at the end of the course.

To Laura, it was okay for her husband to sleep around, but not for her friend to sleep with her husband. I guess I understood, in a weird sort of way.

I sat in the rental car. No, I didn't understand. She could have left Jimmy. Not for a minute did I think I was the only one he fooled around with. But she stayed. Until she knew she couldn't get what she wanted from the bargain, and only then did she leave—him, me, the world. No, I didn't understand at all.

I drove to the town fifteen miles west of the hospital without passing another car on the highway. I wasn't surprised. There was no happening scene in my hometown, not anymore. I crossed the railroad tracks just a few miles before ending up in the downtown area where I spent every weekend of my high school life driving up and down the strip. Cruising was still cool in the 1980s, or at least I told myself it was. The streets were empty tonight. The country was still reeling from the attacks in New York. Parents were still holding their children that much tighter; their children—even those old enough to drive—were clinging them right back.

I drove for several blocks, looking at the darkened storefronts. Nearly three thousand people had died in New York City—three times the population of my hometown. I turned down street after street, but they were all empty, desolate. Relics of my youth, and I was just a visitor now. I turned the car back to the highway.

I pulled onto the shoulder and stared at the railroad tracks that scarred the paved road. The headlights cut through the darkness with ease. I looked out the window, my eyes running back and forth along the road. There were no skid marks. I thought again of the people jumping from the towers, choosing one horrific death over another.

I told people I cried that night, after returning to the hotel, but in truth I had no tears to cry. I was disheartened by the thought that I would never be able to mend my friendship with Laura, but I couldn't be sad. She made her choice, and I respected that.

Laura had jumped too.

SHE WOULD

She slammed through the door and down the front steps, refusing to turn around and yell another obscenity at The Bastard. She would leave for good this time. She got in her truck, revved it into life, and shuddered it out of the gravel driveway and onto the street. The music was cranked, and she rolled down the window to share it with the neighborhood. They would all know. She was leaving. She would show him.

She would leave, get out of this lonely situation, leave him alone with his own damned dishes to clean. She drove to the stop sign at the end of the street. She could go east, toward her mother's, the way she always went when she and The Bastard had a fight, the only two places she had ever been in her life, her mother's house and The Bastard's. Her mother would tell her how stupid she was for leaving a good man, a man with a job and a house and so what if he didn't clean up every once in a while or take her out to the movies on her birthday because he was working. He worked a full-time job. He had a paycheck and was stable, and her mother would tell her to go back and beg forgiveness for her childish reactions.

Or she could go west, out of town, following the dirt road through the farmland. Eventually, hopefully, she would find another road that led somewhere else, then a highway, and then the interstate if she was lucky, and who knows what beyond. She looked to the horizon and saw a storm cloud that seemed to have exploded from the tops of the trees, crisp darkening clouds etched into the blue sky, lightning bouncing around playfully in its core of fiery pinks and yellows that arched upward and clawed their way west, urging her, begging her to take them where they could not go themselves.

She cranked the wheel to the right and headed down the dirt road. She would find her freedom. She would find her own place and her own life, away from someone else's crappy all-we-do-is-sleep-eat-piss of a life. She would do *something*. She would.

She would head west until she found that interstate—she knew there had to be one somewhere, and if she couldn't find it, she would ask. She wouldn't be afraid or nervous. This was her chance! The chance she never knew she wanted but damn if she didn't feel her body tingling with a sense of relief and excitement. Finally she would do what she never knew she wanted to do, and whatever it was, it would be glorious. She would use that word every day: *glorious*. It was not a word she had reason to use now. No, not now, *before*, in her *previous* life. Yes, she would refer to everything—The Bastard, her mother, her life—as *previous*. It was her past, she would not return. She let out a yelp and sang with the music as loud as she could. The Bastard would always tease her, tell her that her singing voice was like a constipated cow, and would turn up the music and tell her to sing louder to see if the other cows reacted. She promised herself that she would sing every day, to every song that came on the radio, even when she didn't know the words to the song. And she would do it loud.

She would drive to the interstate and head further west, further away from her small no-name town. She would keep heading west, taking her fiery storm clouds with her, until there was nothing but sunshine and smiles. And then she would head further west just to be sure, just to be even farther from The Bastard and her mother and that whole previous life. Previous life, it just tasted good when she said it.

While she headed west, she would stop and see the country, everything she had missed growing up in her no-name town. No, it wasn't her no-name town, not anymore. In *that* no-name town. She would stop and see everything she had heard about on the radio or on TV when The Bastard had let her watch something other than ESPN. She would eat at fancy restaurants, the kind with hundreds of items to choose from on their salad bar. She couldn't imagine a salad bar that big. She would go to a spa and have a massage, a real one that felt good and relaxed her. And the whole time she would think of The Bastard and how he would be crying because he didn't have anybody to wash the crap out of his underwear or cook his meals for him or listen to his stories about the guys at work. She would be a tourist in every city and go to see the arch in St. Louis and the Alamo in Texas. She would drive all the way to the Grand Canyon, a giant hole in the earth that she had seen pictures of. She would talk to all the people standing on edge of the Grand Canyon, asking them why they came to see it. She would listen to their stories of beauty and strength and remind them that it was just a hole in the ground, and they would still be in awe, as would she that something so common, so ordinary as a hole in the ground could be made wondrous and exotic by the people who came to see it. She would follow these people back to their hometowns so she would be surrounded by such loving people every day.

A rock from the dirt road pinged off her windshield. She looked for a crack, but found none. She could see another road crossing hers up ahead. She hoped it wasn't a dirt road, she hated dirt roads. She would never live on one again. When she followed the loving people back to their homes, she would not live on a dirt road. She would find a little house on the edge of their neighborhoods and decorate it the way she wanted, whether it was practical not, not like her mother's house, where everything—furniture, floors, dishes—could be wiped down with a damp sponge and the chores would be considered done. She would have a quaint house, a small house where neighbors stopped to visit and she gave them homemade lemonade. She would have a vegetable garden and a bench outside under the tree and a puppy who would chase butterflies in the yard.

And she would find somebody else to share her bed at night. She would have to. She couldn't sleep alone, not anymore. It had been too long. She wouldn't be used to being alone. When the bastard went out late with his buddies, she would try to sleep, but she would have dreams, horrible nightmares, dreams with blood and chasing and falling and drowning, and she would wake up sweating and convinced someone was there in the room with her, preparing to kill her. But when the bastard came home, he would crawl into bed and wrap his huge arms around her and she would feel protected and would sleep peacefully. She never had bad dreams when he slept with her. She rarely had enough covers either. She would have to find someone else to protect her while she slept.

She would have to get a job to pay for her new little house and her garden and her playful puppy. She had never worked before, in her other life. She had barely finished high school when the bastard had taken her home with him, and she had been there for the last seven years. He had always doled out the money for groceries and clothes and anything else she asked for. He had never said no when she asked for money. Maybe her new protector would be the same.

He would be worried, sitting back home, thinking about how she had disappeared. He would call her mother when she didn't return after an hour or two, and then the police when her mother said she hadn't seen her. He would file a missing person's report, search for her. He wouldn't expect that she had just left, taken off, done anything but what she would normally do in these situations, when they fought about the dishes piling up in the sink or him watching football every Sunday instead of enjoying the world outside or her forgetting to pay the cable bill and letting them shut it off. She hadn't meant to. The bill had fallen behind the desk and she just assumed she had already paid it. He would understand that eventually, once he cooled down enough from missing his Sunday football and having to pay the reconnect fee. He would cool down and understand it was just a mistake, an honest mistake, and then he would take her out for ice cream and they would laugh about it. It would be a forced laugh, but he would try, and she would never mention it again.

She would call him when she found a phone, maybe the road ahead would lead to a gas station with a phone, and let him know that she was all right, let him know that she was leaving but she was all right. He would ask her to come back. He wouldn't beg, he never did that, but he would ask, plain and simple, direct and matter of fact, would she come back to him. And when she said no, he would accept it, no cursing or crying or screaming or arguing, and he would say that if she ever needed anything, she could call him. He would say that he would let her mother know because he knew that she wouldn't want to have that discussion with her mother. He understood that theirs was a relationship of necessity and nothing more. And he would help her out this one last time by being the buffer when she needed him.

She came to the crossroad and stopped, trying to guess which way to head, left or right, south toward the Gulf of

Mexico or north toward Canada. *When she needed him.* He would be there when she needed him, even if she wasn't there with him. He would still take care of her in his own way even when she had left him, had abandoned him, had taken her truck, the truck he bought her because she'd seen it on the lot and commented that it was such a deep color of green, the exact color of green that she had always loved. He would do the thing that she was too coward to do herself: tell her mother that she left. And he would do it without her asking him to. He would just know and would tell her that he would take care of it for her.

She looked down the crossroad in both directions, inhaling the aroma of nearby honeysuckle bushes and seeing nothing but farmland—farms she knew were full of tobacco plants and potato plants and some even had apples on then if the kudzu hadn't overgrown the area. They were the producers of the big companies, forgotten out here in the middle of nowhere, empty and soulless yet always working and producing their crops for mass consumption.

She cranked the steering wheel to the left, turning and turning until she was heading back to him. The storm cloud was becoming fuzzy and gray, the yellows not so sharp, the pinks not so bright. She waited for the playful lightning, but it didn't bounce anymore. He would be there when she needed him. She didn't expect any other protector could give her that much. She would go back to him and tell him that she wanted to see the Grand Canyon and he would take her, maybe next summer, and she would clean his underwear and pay the bills and know that he was there for her, whenever she needed him. She would watch the horizon for other storm clouds, and the next time one started forming, she would go inside, lock her doors, watch football with him, and remind herself that he was there for her when she needed him. She would.

OPEN SESAME

The train whistle sounded as his fingers brushed at my shoulder. Maybe he was brushing at my hair. Maybe he just wanted to touch me one last time. His fingers were gentle, pausing briefly on my shoulder. I fought the urge to recoil.

"I need to get on the train, Alex," I said, looking up slightly into his face. He was looking at a thin strand of my auburn hair that he had captured between his fingers. He didn't want to listen to me. I stepped back, pulling my hair from his fingers, pulling his attention back to the present.

"I have something to show you." His voice was barely audible above the sounds on the platform, workers loading the cars, mothers trying to keep their children and luggage in tow, lovers sharing tearful goodbyes on the cold Russian evening. And then there was us.

I cocked my head, curious, then chastised myself, certain it was all an excuse. He put his cigarette in his mouth, took of his coat and shoved it between his knees, then used both hands to pull down the front of his flannel shirt. A flash of white t-shirt appeared, and he reached further and scooped both shirts together. He looked at me, waiting.

I scowled, unsure what he was showing me. I shook my head at the small picture just above his heart. A tattoo of a seven-pointed star, etched in blue, surrounding a second golden star. I tried to look away, furious, but couldn't take my eyes from the star. I leaned forward about to reach out to it, touch it, caress it.

A train whistle blew. Passengers hurried past us. I fought the urge to explore the star with my fingers. I stepped closer, but it was gone. Alex let go of his shirts and quickly tucked them into his jeans. He shrugged into his coat and took the cigarette from between his lips.

"I knew you would like it. He did a good job, yes?" Alex grinned and blew smoke out and up into the air.

I took a deep breath. Deep breaths are supposed to be calming. Everyone says so. I took a deeper breath, but I wasn't calming down. *What the fuck do people know?* I let the fire erupt inside of me and gripped the straps of my backpack until I had no feeling in my hands. I knew if I let go of the straps, I would hit him. I would hit him hard and fast and probably more than once. I craved the satisfaction of punching my fist right into his smug smile. One time wouldn't be enough. Maybe two or three punches. Maybe ten or twenty.

"You stupid son of a bitch." I didn't scream or yell. I didn't need to. I took a step closer, making it difficult for him to look down at me without pulling back. "Is this some stupid way of trying to get us back together?" I poked him once where the star was hiding, digging my fingernail through his layers of clothes. It felt good, but not good enough. "Don't you get it, you stupid bastard?" I kept poking, wondering just how tender the new tattoo was. "I'm leaving so I never have to see dumb asses like you!"

He fell back a few steps, his eyes wild. "I know you're leaving."

Obviously I wasn't reacting the way he had hoped. He probably expected me to fall into his arms and declare my undying love.

"I wanted to show you how important you are to me." He grabbed my hand and pushed back the cuff of my coat, revealing similar stars embedded on my wrist. "Now I know that we will always share something very special."

I looked at him and was revolted. Had I really spent the last few months with this guy? His was so young. *Jesus, I'm like a friggin' pedophile.* I jerked my hand back and glanced around for the nearest place to discreetly spit up the bread and cheese I had wolfed down before grabbing a taxi to the train station.

"I will never forget how close we were. We will always have this bond of love."

I laughed because I could. Young and naïve. I really knew how to pick them. He looked hurt. I didn't care. I needed to lash out at him, hurt him somehow.

I shook my head in condescension. "Wake up." Then I walked away, leaving the anger behind.

He didn't follow me. I never looked back at him, but I knew he was there. I was annoyed that he had interrupted my last moments in the city.

I climbed on the train, found my compartment, and piled my things in the storage area. I heaved a sigh and collapsed on the seat, leaning back against the wall and looking at the poorly lit room, trying to ignore the grime the weak light was trying to hide. My traveling companion arrived, nodding and greeting me as he secured his bags.

Oliver was a friend of a friend of a friend…or something like that. We met briefly once at a company party. He came as a guest, but I couldn't make the connection now. I just remember his escort being blonde. And from the travel office. I shrugged.

We sat in silence, listening to the sounds of the train getting ready to depart the station. I looked out the window and saw people congregating around a dim street light, waiting to make sure the train left. The sun had disappeared behind the station building. Soon it would be completely dark. I could still see Alex's cigarette burning as he drew heavily on it. He stood near the circle of people, but out of reach of the street light.

Passengers looking for their places walked back and forth in the corridor outside our compartment, yelling and shouting in celebration when they were successful. Others yelled at the conductor, complaining about their compartments.

Oliver reached up and slid the door until it was almost completely closed. "Maybe we will be lucky. Maybe we will be alone in the room." He nodded to the empty berths across from us. The tiny compartment had four berths, two below and two above, separated by a small table connected to the wall beneath the dirty window.

I smiled. "Yeah, that would be nice." *But I've never been that lucky.*

Oliver nodded and we both lapsed into silence again. I could feel the train shifting as people continued to look for their places, their muffled voices continuing to intrude into our compartment. I looked out the window again. The cigarette moved up and down in its established rhythm.

The train jerked, and I thought we were finally leaving. I sat up on the edge of the berth, but nothing happened.

"It is probably an old woman loading her merchandise for the market," Oliver said. He laughed, then peered through the small crack left by the door. I sighed and threw myself back against the wall again. I was anxious to get away from the glowing ember.

The voices in the corridor quieted as people settled down for the overnight trip. Suddenly the train moved forward violently, ripping itself from the station. I watched out the window, staring at the scenery we had yet to pass. I didn't want to see the darkened buildings of St. Petersburg, the architectural capital of Russia, and be reminded of the little grocery store where I had found cheap bottled Pepsi and the bewildered look on the cashier's face when I told her I wanted 24 bottles. I rubbed my shoulder thinking about how I had loaded them into my backpack for the hour-long trek back to my apartment, where Alex had ended up drinking most of them. I didn't want to think about the Neva River, where Alex and I walked during White Nights, celebrating the dusty light horizon at midnight. We ended up being trapped in the center of the city when, at 2 am, all the bridges along the twisted river were raised and we had no escape to the suburbs. We wandered the inner city, holding hands and sneaking private moments, until the subway system opened the next morning. I wanted to forget these memories, now tainted by the feeling that he had stolen something from me, something core to my being.

"Tickets!" The conductor threw open the door, letting the outside noises in. I jerked forward, looking at the intruder. "Hey, girl, where are your tickets?" He asked in Russian, looking at me sternly. Oliver quickly produced two small pieces of paper with lists of numbers. The conductor took the tickets and looked at the other berths. "These are free, eh?"

Oliver motioned for him to move into the corridor, then spoke to him in Russian. Just before I turned to the window, I saw Oliver pull several bills from his pocket. A few more exchanges, then Oliver reentered the compartment, firmly shutting the door behind him. He sat down on the opposite berth and smiled. "No problem."

I shook my head and pulled out my money. "How much did you pay him?"

He shook his head and insisted he had paid nothing.

"I am not stupid. I saw you give him money."

Oliver smiled and winked. "It's no problem. When I bought my ticket, the cashier was too busy chatting up his girlfriend." He chuckled. "I gave him a thousand ruble note to pay for the tickets and he gave me 1300 rubles in change." Oliver shrugged, then looked out the window. "I was just spreading my good fortune around a bit with the conductor. He gets some extra pocket change, and we don't have to worry about drunk Russians in the middle of the night—and I am still traveling for free!"

I laughed. "Man, where was I when the cashier became distracted?"

"Busy talking to that boy."

I half glanced at Oliver to see if there was any hint of condescension in his use of the word *boy*. But I immediately reminded myself that Alex was a boy—not biologically, but mentally. He was actually a few years older than I was, and when we first started dating, I was so excited about finally being with someone mature.

I snorted at the thought.

Oliver gave me a questioning look, but I just shook my head. "You will miss him," he said.

I laughed, startling him. "Oh no, that will not be an issue."

He raised one eyebrow at me.

"Stop it," I said, all laughter gone. "You don't even know the half of it." I clasped my hands together on my lap, my thumb rubbing the opposite wrist, moving back and forth over the blue and gold stars.

"We have all night." Oliver spread his hands before him. "Plenty of time to explain it to me."

I rolled my eyes and crossed my arms.

"Okay, you wait here, consider what you want to share." He stood up. "I will return in just one moment." He pulled open the door, the sounds from the corridor crashing into the compartment. He glanced both ways, then stepped through the door before turning to slide it shut, offering me a reassuring wink before disappearing behind the closed door.

I wasn't sure what to make of Oliver. I had spoken to him once after the party, on the phone. The train was taking me to Tallinn, Estonia, where I had twenty-two-hour wait before my flight. I didn't know the city very well. The girl from travel mentioned that Oliver was originally from Tallinn, so I called for some suggestions. He immediately offered to escort me, saying his parents were pressuring him to come for a visit. Traveling with me meant he could visit quickly and have a built-in excuse for leaving that his mother couldn't ignore. Travel girl told me that he checked out, was a decent guy.

But now he wanted me to tell him about my broken love life. I felt my walls going up, brick by brick. And we would be alone, all night, in a locked compartment. What if he didn't really check out?

I took a long breath to slow my heart, chastising myself. None of my warning signs had gone off until I let my imagination have free rein. I looked out the window again, staring into the blackness as the train moved into the Russian countryside.

Someone knocked on the door. Three rapid knocks followed by three slow ones, then three more rapid ones. I tugged on the handle and slid the door open a crack. Oliver was on the other side, two tall glasses of steaming tea resting in metal holders.

He smiled. "Abracadabra—no, wait, I mean open sesame."

I pulled the door open and moved back to the table under the window, clearing off hip pack and gloves to make room for the tea. I rummaged around in my pack for some Kleenex, then used two tissues to wipe down the table as best I could, sliding the tea glasses first one way, then the other.

Oliver had the storage compartment open, looking through his bags. He pulled several small wrapped packages from different bags, set them on the table, then closed the compartment and sat down. He unwrapped a loaf of Russian brown bread, a small salami roll, several hard-boiled eggs, a large chunk of white cheese, and a small bag of spicy cabbage salad. I pulled two packages of cookies and a chocolate bar from my bag and dropped them on the table.

"Dessert," I said.

Oliver frowned. "No, something is not right." He stood up again to go through his bags once more. He was not planning on staying Tallinn long, so I wondered about the bags. Then I remembered him mentioning that his mother had a standing order of goods she wanted from Russia because they were so much cheaper than in Estonia.

"Aha!" Oliver said and straightened from his search. He turned to show me two bottles of Russian champagne. I laughed. "My girlfriend bought them for my mother." He shook his head. "She doesn't drink, she will never know. Just one more thing."

He left the compartment again. I found my army knife in my hip pack and began slicing salami and cheese. He returned with two large plastic cups, obviously confiscated from the conductor's private stash.

"Now, we feast!"

"Do I even want to know how much you had to pay the conductor for those?" I nodded at the plastic cups.

He feigned surprise. "Cost? They cost nothing!" He smiled. "It was the least he could do to help a person with your illness."

"Illness?"

Oliver blew on his tea. He glanced at me over the rim of his glass. "Broken heart," he said, then took a few tentative sips.

I stopped cutting, the knife poised above the salami. I almost didn't hear it. I wasn't sure I had heard it correctly.

He set his tea down and rearranged the food on the table. "Broken heart. I told him you had to leave your lover in Russia and go home to America. I told him you don't want to leave, but your parents want you to marry an American." He glanced up and smiled. "He understood. He thinks it is romantic. Sad, but romantic." He tore a chunk of bread off the loaf, picked up a piece of salami, and popped both into his mouth. He sat back against the berth, chewing the bread and salami as he watched the darkness outside the window pass by.

I nibbled on the cheese as I drank my tea, afraid that if I ate too much everything would come right back up again. Oliver's comments had stirred my memories again, and flashes of Alex carrying my groceries down the street, standing in line to buy tickets to a movie that turned out to be a porn spoof of Robin Hood, and racing out the door late to work after a quickee in the shower all morphed into a swirling vortex of him standing on the platform, smoking his cigarette, and showing off his tattoo.

My tattoo. I drank the hot tea in several gulps, trying to burn out the foul taste in my mouth. It was a taste of misunderstanding, of deception, of violation. Yes, violated. That was the word. Alex—in his "it's all about my feelings" demonstration—had violated me. I slammed the glass down, cracking the bottom against the metal holder.

"Oh, crap!" I grabbed the tissues to clean up the remaining tea that drizzled from the bottom of the glass. "That was stupid," I mumbled.

Oliver watched from hooded eyes. I was glad that he didn't seem to be interested in my embarrassing show of emotion. I placed the now-empty glass in one of the plastic bags that had held the food and set it by the door, sure that I would be paying the conductor for that mishap in the morning.

Oliver finished off the rest of his tea. "Perhaps it is best we move on to the second course." He grabbed one of the bottles of champagne and unwrapped the foil from the bottle's neck.

"Oh, I think I've already had too much to drink. Can't you tell?" I pointed to the broken glass and smiled.

Oliver made a *tsking* sound with his tongue, shook his head once, and kept opening the bottle. The plastic cork suddenly popped and triumph spread across his face, lighting up his dark eyes. He grabbed a plastic cup as the bottle overflowed. "I think this is the course we should have started with."

He set the cup down in front of me and licked the champagne off his fingers before filling the second cup. He raised his cup in the air, waiting for the toast.

"To friends," I said. I started to drink, but he placed his hand on my arm to stop me.

He scowled. "This is not a good toast." He raised his cup again and waited for me to do the same. "I wish you health, wealth, and happiness. May you always have good friends and true love." He smiled briefly, then drank the entire cup of champagne.

I forced a tight smile, wished him the same, and followed suit. We each ate a cookie in silence before he poured the second round.

He lifted his cup. "To wonderful adventures, travels around the world, and just a hint of trouble." He threw back his champagne in one gulp and waited for me to do the same. He made a goofy smile and crossed his eyes until I drank my champagne.

My body warmed with lightness. I grabbed a second cookie. Oliver collected the cups and poured the third round, emptying the remainder of the first bottle. He put the empty bottle on the floor and moved the second bottle to the table. "Never leave an empty bottle on table. It means the end of the party. Ah, soon we will open the second bottle."

"I'll make the toast this time," I said, raising my cup. "To our families, who support us and make everything possible." It took several swallows to finish the third cup.

"Too bad you will not have time to meet my mother. I think she would like you." Oliver worked on opening the second bottle of champagne. "So, what will you do in America?"

I thought for a moment, blushing. "I know it sounds weird, but the first thing? Play with my dog. I miss him the most, ya know?" I looked to see if he understood. "I mean,

I've talked to my parents a lot since I've been here, but you can't really talk to the dog."

The cork popped out and he poured another round, nodding.

I inhaled deeply, slowly. "We're drinking this stuff way too fast. My head is already spinning."

He looked offended, but I knew it was just an act. "Your last night in Russia and you won't celebrate with me? Terrible, just terrible." He shook his head. "Look at it this way: You do not have to drive home tonight. Just lie down and good night." He motioned to the berth I sat on. I decided being tipsy would be a good way to help ignore the cockroaches that were bound to come out once the light went off.

"Okay, but after this one, we take a break."

He nodded. "But you must promise to drink the whole cup, yes?"

I agreed, anything to get it over with. I watched him fill the cups to the rim, emptying more than two-thirds of the champagne bottle.

"Oh, cheap shot!" I said, laughing. "You want me to be hung over tomorrow?" I stuck out my tongue and rolled my eyes, mimicking a hangover.

He laughed. "Very beautiful. Now I know why he loves you so much."

I pushed the cup away, splashing champagne over the table. "Don't. Just don't." I leaned back against the berth. "You have no idea, anyway."

He shrugged and sat back as well. He stared at me from his side of the compartment, and I stared back. This was not an argument that he was going to win. He didn't know Alex. He didn't know how exhausting it was to have to explain everything to Alex, who had never traveled, had never gone to school, had never had a job except taking care of his mother's apartment buildings. She paid him well, and he made the kinds of connections necessary that enabled him to buy his own apartment building. He was building his life, and that would be enough for most women.

But not me. I wanted the romance and the security. I wanted intelligence and playfulness. I wanted spontaneity and a workaholic. And when my contract for the company ended, it offered the perfect opportunity to cut the ties cleanly and move on to the next adventure, where I could find another plaything until it was time to move on again.

Shit. I looked away from Oliver's dark eyes. Commitment was not my strong point. I told myself it was just because I hadn't found Mr. Right, but I held my wrist and knew it was a lie.

I sat forward. "Ok, let's do this." I picked up my cup carefully, trying not to spill too much, and waited for the toast. When he didn't say anything, I decided to make the toast and get it over with. "I wish you a long life with the love of your life, and I hope you have a bunch of kids to keep you happy!" He smiled, and I drank to the toast. When I finished, I noticed his cup was still full. "What, you're not going to drink to your own happiness? Isn't that bad luck or something?"

"I will drink, after I make a toast for you." He lifted his cup a notch, looking surprisingly sober. "I wish you not to be afraid to love. I wish you to be strong, to stay with the one you love. I wish you not to run away." I watched him drink, shocked by his words.

"What does that mean?" My voice was just a whisper, but I knew he heard me.

He wasn't looking at me. He was tracing the rim of his cup with his forefinger. "You love that boy." He said it quietly, continuing to watch his finger. "We all see it. But you left him. You love him, so you decide to leave?"

His eyes raised to meet mine and I was momentarily lost in his dark gaze.

"We dated. It didn't work out. We broke up." It sounded as flat and rehearsed as an explanation could be.

He turned his head slightly, not taking his eyes off me.

The shock wore off, and the anger returned. "Why do you care? I don't even know you." I crossed my arms and scowled at him. I was tired of his psycho-analysis.

He was shaking his head when he spoke again. "You travel around the world searching—what are you searching for?" He leaned forward to accentuate his words.

"How would you like it if I asked about your relationships?" I grabbed the bottle of champagne and filled my cup. I didn't offer him any. He didn't ask. "For example, when you are going to marry your girlfriend? She is trying to get in good with your mother, so clearly she thinks it is going somewhere." I drank the champagne quickly and looked to him for an answer.

He leaned back, sighing. "I ask, she says no. I will wait." He looked out the window. "One day she will say yes. I will be there when she does." I waited for him to continue. "It is very hard to wait, but I will. I love her. I will not love another."

I was touched by his sincerity and suddenly I felt like a jerk for being so defensive. I dropped my head into my hands and instantly regretted it. The dizziness in my head was intensified by the movement of the train. I slowly lay down on the seat and covered my eyes with my arm. I listened to the rhythm of the train on its rails. The sound was mesmerizing, and I found myself relaxing into it.

"I asked someone to marry me once." Even after I said it, I didn't believe I had spoken the words aloud. I waited for a reaction, but got none. I rolled my head to look at him. He sat looking at me, waiting. I looked back to the ceiling. "He said no, obviously." I waited again, listening to the *clickity-clack* of the train.

"Is he the one?"

I looked back across the compartment. "What do you mean?"

"The one who hurt you so badly that you do not get close to people now."

I looked at the ceiling and thought about it. I thought about the relationship in my youth that I had felt so strongly about. What was it that I loved about that guy? I tried to think about one quirk, one action that I remembered fondly. My mind was blank.

"No. I didn't really love him."

"Then why did you ask him to marry you?" His voice echoed the question my own mind was posing. I rolled on to my side and propped my head on my hand.

"I guess it felt like the thing to do. Meet a guy, date him for a while, get married, have kids. End of story." I chewed on my lip. "Pretty sad story, huh?"

He glanced at my exposed wrist. "What's that for?"

I lifted my head to look at my wrist and immediately regretted it. My head felt like it weighed a ton, and I plopped it back down on my hand. "A reminder."

"Of what?"

I dropped my head down to the cushion and held out my arm so he could see the dual stars on my wrist. "Seven-seven, see?"

He nodded.

I rolled onto my back, pulling my arm to my chest. "I think it's late. I need to get some sleep. Tomorrow will be difficult." I wanted the movement of the train to seduce me to sleep. I closed my eyes and thought about it moving through the countryside.

I heard him get up and turn off the overhead light. I pretended to sleep, although my mind was racing, bringing back thoughts of the failed relationships in my past. I tried to remember how the relationships had started, how they had blossomed, but I could only focus on how they had deteriorated. They had all been good guys, friendly and caring, but none had seemed right. Jeremiah with the deep amber eyes and eternal light-hearted mood had been surprised and confused at the abrupt ending. Intelligent and sweet, Zach had been angry, arguing with me during the entire breakup. Alex had just looked at me with those big sad eyes. The first was David, with the light southern drawl and the endearing qualities I just couldn't seem to remember. David, who had painfully broken my heart with his rejection. We had stayed together for a few more months after I proposed, but it was never the same. In the end he left me since I didn't have the courage to walk away. I left everybody after him. It was self-preservation. Dump them before they could dump me. Avoid the rejection.

"It's the rejection." I knew he was awake. I didn't have to look at him. He heard me. "I'm never good enough." I heard him roll over, but I still couldn't look at him. "Even for my son." The champagne was churning in my stomach, moving in time with the *clickity-clack* of the train. "The stars—seven, seven. He died July 7, three weeks before he was supposed to be born."

I waited for him to speak. I waited for the encouraging words, the ones that would tell me that it's not my fault. I waited for him to reassure me and comfort me. I waited for him to tell me that they weren't rejecting me, that my son hadn't rejected me even before he was born. I waited and listened.

But all I heard was the train's metal wheels spinning on the track.

THE HONEYSUCKLE CONNECTION

When I was in first and second grade, my family lived in an enormous city in the south. My memories of that city are crowded with cars honking and people talking incessantly. I just remember noise. But there was also a place a few blocks from my house that we would get to by crossing through an apartment complex's parking lot. Here the river channel was surrounded by honeysuckle bushes, and we would pick the flowers from the bushes and suck on the sweet nectar. It was a haven of calm while the world raged on "out there."

Those honeysuckle bushes are long gone, but the feelings they evoked remain with me and often peek through in my writing. The stories in the Honeysuckle series focus on people dealing with some intense emotions as they face changes at the core of who they are. Some rage against the changes being forced on them, others embrace the changes, but somewhere along the way, they have a fleeting moment of detachment, a brief interlude when they too are able to enjoy the honeysuckle nectar.

ABOUT THE AUTHOR

C. Jai Ferry grew up in a small rural town in one of those middle states between New York and Los Angeles. She focuses on short stories with narrators who are often described as brutally honest and who likely need some form of professional help. If you've enjoyed these stories, please leave a review. Thank you!

Check out all of C. Jai Ferry's novels, short stories, and ebooks as well as free stories and what's coming next by visiting www.cjaiferry.com.

www.ingramcontent.com/pod-product-compliance
Lightning Source LLC
Chambersburg PA
CBHW020629250626
47154CB00004B/1736